Rear-View Mirror

Rear-View Mirror

Caroline B. Cooney

Random House
New York

Library of Congress Cataloging in Publication Data
Cooney, Caroline B
Rear-view mirror.
I. Title.
PZ4.C7758Re [PS3553.O578] 813'.5'4 79-5544
ISBN 0-394-51054-2

Manufactured in the United States of America

24689753

First Edition

for John Goodwin

Rear-View Mirror

Prologue

T HE farmyard was quiet except for a German shepherd pacing back and forth in its wire run. The little phony Colonial brick ranch sat incongruously right in the lap of a falling-in, unpainted old frame house. It had been years—presumably the lifetime of the brick ranch—since anyone had put any energy into the collapsing gray frame house. Its windows were gone, its front porch sagging. An old refrigerator and a broken space heater decorated the doorway.

A few hundred yards to the west were several old barns and sheds. No one moved near them. No engines droned, no voices broke the hot October morning. Tire marks had worn away the grass in the front yard of the ranch, but there was no car parked there now.

Jerry Sam Hopps stood behind the trunk of the last pine tree in the deep woods that ringed the farm. His lungs heaved, sucking in hot humid air. His muscles were trembling. Not home, thought Jerry Sam, waiting for his pounding heart to slow down. They ain't nobody at home.

He wondered if they had missed him yet at the Correctional Facility. He hadn't planned the escape; it had more or less fallen into his lap. Jerry Sam had been the only one to see the opportunity. He'd slipped into the woods and begun to run. Years before, someone had planted those pines in neat, square order. Depending on the angle at which you stood, they were either dizzyingly symmetrical or an impenetrable maze. Jerry Sam had thought the running would be easy because no scrub growth could thrive beneath the thick shade of the trees, but the slim dry whips of the lower branches had torn at his face and clothes. Even though he'd run with his hands up like fenders around the rubber tire of his face, it was painfully scratched.

From the pines he had emerged in swamp, the low ugly carcass of the backwoods of the Carolinas. Jerry Sam was a country boy; neither lowlands or snakes scared him. He was afraid only of dogs. The prison had bloodhounds. By now they'd be snuffling in the woods, pulling eagerly on their leads. He had no time to waste.

The farmhouse had a German shepherd. What kind of protection did the stupid farmer think a penned-up dog was going to give him?

Jerry Sam took a final deep breath and walked up to the kitchen door of the brick ranch. The dog went berserk in its pen, barking, growling, attacking through the heavy wire mesh. Jerry Sam thumbed his nose at it.

The kitchen door was not locked.

He walked in, grinning to himself. Typical country. Y'all come see us now, door ain't never closed.

He had to get out of his prison garb. He hoped the farmer wasn't some huge beer-bellied slob whose clothes wouldn't fit.

Kicking off the wet ruined shoes that had dragged him through the mud and creeks, he went down the narrow hall to the bedrooms. They had a son, and the son was in high school, and the son was into skateboarding. Jerry Sam sneered. A kid who played dumb-ass games when there was a world out there to be whipped. At least the kid had plenty of blue jeans.

Jerry Sam pulled on a pair, found that they fit somewhat, picked out socks, sneakers—too large; he added another pair of socks—and a shirt. The kid had nice shirts. He took a T-shirt with wide red and navy stripes and a fat white tab collar. Class. Then he ripped off all the skateboarding posters the kid had Scotch-taped to his walls. He tried to smash the skateboard, but it was some kind of thick plastic; probably you could run over it with a Mack truck and not hurt it.

Back in the kitchen, he decided he needed something to eat. Running gave a man an appetite. But all there was was cereal. And it wasn't even sugar cereal. If there was one thing Jerry Sam hated, it was plain cereal. Like prison, where they had oatmeal and grits, but no sugar and no butter. He cursed the stupid little pellets of wheat and hurled the box across the room. It decapitated a little plant growing on the window sill, which was gratifying. Then he smashed all the dishes drying on the counter by the sink so the stupid farmer's wife would know just how much he hated cereal that wasn't sugar-coated.

The blue jeans began to fall down over his slim hips. He'd have to get a belt. He stomped back to the kid's room and stepped right on the skateboard. Jerry Sam's feet flew out from under him. His arms flailed, but all he got for that effort was a hard crack on his elbow against the bureau. The base of his spine hit the floor first.

When he could stand up again, he spent the next fifteen minutes smashing everything in the house that he could pick up and swing.

Feeling better, he hitchhiked into Cross Hill, where it would be easy to steal a car. Jerry Sam had never walked anywhere in his life. The soles of his feet were made for pressing accelerators.

The trucker who gave him a lift was the inquisitive type, so Jerry Sam said he had missed the bus for high school. This pleased the trucker, who liked to frown over the evils of busing, and he detoured to drop Jerry Sam right in front of Cross River High. That was fine with Jerry Sam. He summoned his cousin Powell from second-period history class —now that was fun, sauntering into old Miss Melchior's room and letting her see who was boss these days—and together they decided on a hamburger joint as the best place to find a car.

It was a little early, though, and the selection was limited. Only three cars had their keys in the ignition. One was one of those tiny new things with an engine so small you couldn't pass a limping dog. The owner of the second came out of the restaurant just as Jerry Sam was getting to the driver's door of his car, so they were left with an old white station wagon some out-of-state jerks had left idling. "The world," said Jerry Sam, who felt there was much to teach Powell; Powell was what you might call a slow learner, "is full of fools." The car wasn't too bad. Old, but a nice solid V-8 with automatic transmission that could really take charge of the road. Especially in the countryside, where there weren't even traffic lights to cramp Jerry Sam's style, it would be a good car.

He and Powell held up a gas station down the road just by talking rough, and got forty-six dollars. Now *that* was being boss. You only had to look at them and they shriveled up and gave you money.

Still, he'd feel better with a gun.

They went back to the farmhouse to get the shotgun he'd seen leaning against the pantry wall. Powell shot the German shepherd, which was practically killing itself anyway, biting at the wire mesh in an effort to stop the second intrusion of the hour.

After that Jerry Sam and Powell simply cruised, with no particular plan other than to enjoy themselves. The car radio didn't work, so Jerry Sam shot it out.

"We could drive down to the shopping mall in Nearing River," said Powell. "We got enough money from the gas station to buy us a radio that works."

Jerry Sam liked that. He could listen to the news about his escape. They kept to back roads in case any cops were looking for Jerry Sam. But even to natives, the flat boring countryside, with its collapsing tobacco barns and patches of wood and shorn field, had no landmarks. With very little effort Jerry Sam and Powell got themselves lost.

But that, as Jerry Sam pointed out, was just as well.

Something had turned up in the back seat of the station wagon that needed disposal.

One

O CTOBER, a car—and an excuse to drive. That, thought Susan Seton, ranks right up there with bread, wine and thou.

A sign loomed blue and white by the edge of the highway:

FOOD GAS

Since she still had a half-dozen doughnut holes in the white paper bag beside her and the fuel tank was more than two-thirds full, FOOD GAS had little appeal. But she turned off anyhow because she didn't want to be on a highway—was there only by accident in the first place—and the name of the exit road was Rose of Sharon Church Slope.

Any road with a name like that, Susan told herself, has to be worth exploring. Weedy or not.

Susan did not particularly care about the weeds. Not

today. They were just her excuse to drive for miles under the beautiful Carolina-blue sky.

She yawned, stretching under her seat belt, drifting in a world of soft upholstered car and sunny sky.

The vase. How many weeds would it take to fill that vase?

She'd been given the vase by her mother, who had taken up pottery seriously. Susan had more mugs, serving bowls and planters than any normal human being could break in a lifetime, and when her mother visited the month before, Susan had dreaded it. She would be able to pave the floor in pot shards before long. Especially the way Roger crashed around in the mornings. Of course, more breakfasts than not Roger was out of town, so the odds were growing in favor of the mugs.

The latest creation, however, was a huge round floor vase mottled with rust and brown. An urn suitable for a home-spun genie or an armload of autumn weeds.

Susan opted for weeds. She could see them perfectly, like a slick magazine photograph, beige and golden and brittle yellow, filling the corner of her living room, placed directly under the macramé hanging that had been last winter's pro-ject.

She turned the opposite way from FOOD GAS, which sounded more like asphalt than weeds, and drove slowly, peacefully down Rose of Sharon Church Slope Road.

It had no slope, but she hadn't expected it to. The name, like so many place names in North Carolina, was undoubt-edly Biblical. If there were any hills in eastern North Caro-lina, they were as yet uncharted.

Flat, flat, flat, diagnosed Susan. Like me.

Neither affliction bothered her today. The sky was too blue and the freedom too lovely.

She had gone into Dr. Fiori's office at six forty-five, as usual. After nearly a year of it, Susan was actually awake when she started work. It was a continuing surprise to Susan that Dr. Fiori's vile office hours were a success. Who would have thought all of Nearing River wanted to have its dental appointments early enough to get to work and school on time?

"I've got a cough," said Dr. Fiori, leaning heavily on her desk and managing to look underloved and undernourished. "Thought I could just wear a mask and get through the day, but I can't. I'm at death's door," he said dramatically.

"Does that mean you want me to cancel today?" said Susan.

"What a way you have with words," said the dentist. "By all means. Cancel today."

It took Susan exactly fourteen minutes to cancel Tuesday's patients. Dr. Fiori complimented her on her usual show of efficiency. "It isn't me, it's the hour," she said. "Very few people are far from their telephones at six forty-five in the morning."

Dr. Fiori decided then to take his phone off the hook when he got home and into bed. When he was at death's door he wanted to concentrate on it, and not be interrupted by ringing in his ears.

He paused by the doorway to consider the loss of revenue that today would represent. He could give Gayle and Maribeth, his chairside assistants, the day off without pay. But then they might quit and he would lose time and funds having to train new girls. He would just have to give them the time off and hope it endeared him to them.

Susan was a different matter. She was not only a worker, but he also had her wrapped around his little finger. He envied Roger Seton a wife as dedicated to the Protestant ethic as Susan. He bundled Gayle and Maribeth out the back door and went back to Susan's desk. Putting on his most forlorn expression, he asked her if she would be willing, since he felt so bad, so terribly, terribly bad, to stay and clear up the paperwork. "And when you've done that," he said generously, "why don't you just run along home?"

The prospect of time off loomed warm and wonderful in Susan's eyes. She jerked out the files to be worked on, the bills and reminders to be sent, and whipped through the backlog in two hours flat. It took her one more hour to do the orders that needed to go out (Dr. Fiori was infatuated by color-coded files and cutely named children's favors and boxes of Kleenex with flower arrangements trying to disguise them), and at ten-thirty Susan closed up the office.

Breakfast. A leisurely breakfast, with hashed browns and bacon strips and orange juice. She dawdled, agreeing with the waitress that for the first week in October it certainly was hot.

All Tuesday ahead of me, she thought, wandering out to her car, and three loads of laundry waiting in the apartment in case I do something silly like go home and try to accomplish something.

Across the street the bank sign flashed the temperature. Eighty-four degrees at 11:32. She toyed with the idea of turning on the car radio to find out how high the humidity was, but decided against it. It was high. Period. It would be a typical sweltering fall day. Now. What to do with the rest of it?

She remembered her mother's floor vase and the task of filling the monstrous thing with weeds. A drive. A long, meandering drive through the country in search of milk-weed pods and grass fronds and cattails.

Susan stopped at the doughnut shop, bought a bag of holes in case the hashed browns proved to less filling than they had felt going down, and tucked herself happily under her seat belt, ready to attack a waiting world of weeds.

She hadn't indulged herself in aimless driving since the fuel crisis of '74. She had six years' worth coming to her. That should use up Tuesday.

She was in the middle of nowhere, which befitted a weed hunter. Woods, empty fields, scrubby hedges, a deserted family graveyard, a falling-in, never-painted shack, a pile of rusting cars and more pine woods. She decided to drive by back roads all the way to Raleigh and spend the afternoon at the shopping centers that decorated the capital like so many cement blocks on a Christmas tree. Maybe at a specialty shop she could find a few colorful dried flowers to thread among her field weeds.

She trundled down Rose of Sharon Church Slope until she came to a dirt road. Anyone knew weeds grew better at the sides of dirt roads. HARMONY X RD—6MI   She turned left, jouncing on the ruts left from the last heavy rain.

Mostly pine woods, right up to the ditches on each side of the red clay road, with a sprinkling of dry dusty fields, their crops long gone. On one field, hay had been baled in jelly-roll fashion and the rolls sat in a circle like some temporary Stonehenge. And then around the bend she came to the perfect field. Fallow for several years, it was waist-deep in dried brown and gold weeds, dotted with small green pines eager to absorb the field into the woods.

It even had a slope.

An upward incline for a few hundred yards, and presumably therefore a downward side beyond the weeds.

How exciting, thought Susan. I'm surprised they don't have a marker here by the roadside: THIS SPOT 110 FEET ABOVE SEA LEVEL. I'd rather read that than FOOD GAS any day.

She parked in a dusty farm track that led through the field. Jamming the keys in the pocket of her pants suit—such a clever girl, Susan congratulated herself, wearing an old suit to work today, and not even a double-knit to snag on every stalk—she draped the jacket over the passenger headrest, by-passed a lush stand of black-eyed Susans and strode out into the weeds. She had lifted Dr. Fiori's office scissors to cut her stalks. They glittered in the hot sun.

Janelle and Henry Davenport had saved for four years to go to Disney World and they were doing it right: motels and restaurants all the way. They had tried camping once, but the twins kept crawling out of the tent, Janelle couldn't bring herself to use the latrines, Henry couldn't sleep without his evening shower, and they all hated mosquitoes.

They were taking their time driving south. There was a lot to see. The Chesapeake Bay Bridge and Tunnel—now that was an engineering feat to marvel over. The wind came like armloads of damp salt through the opened windows of their ancient station wagon. On the horizon, the painted silhouettes of freighters moved slowly closer, and among the whitecaps next to the Bridge islands were dozens of sailboats, fishing boats and motorized pleasure craft. In the marsh grasses at the Maryland end they saw several white heron-like birds standing on one leg, bills darting down into the water. "Just like *National Geographic,*" said Henry happily, angling his camera, although the birds were much too far away to show up on his film.

"We'll have to quit the bank," said Janelle. "Go into photography."

"Become travel writers."

They both knew they would never leave the bank. They were totally happy with their jobs. Henry had read *The Peter Principle* with great interest, and at twenty-eight, when his fellow clerks were jostling for positions on the management ladder, turned down a promotion. Income was nice—it was very nice, and the more you had the nicer it got—but he was old enough (having been aged quickly by the arrival of the twins) to appreciate peace of mind as well. He'd stay a teller.

Janelle was permitted to work in the same bank only because she and Henry were in different departments on different floors. She sat from nine to five in the rarefied atmosphere of the trust department on the fifth floor—which meant the air conditioning broke down more often in the summer and the carpet was cleaned more often in the winter—and wrote checks. She had an orderly mind and flawless typing ability, and she too turned down promotions. She liked writing checks. Trust recipients were very interesting. Sometimes you paid for mundane things like their rent or their Bloomingdale's charge for pantyhose or their children's braces. Sometimes you arranged trips to exotic islands, though, or ordered cases of liquor for big impressive parties with equally exotic themes or paid for traffic tickets acquired from consuming aforesaid liquor. Janelle knew the trust families intimately, although she had rarely laid eyes on any of them. She was intensely fond of some, tolerant of the others, and only really disliked one particular family.

Going down into the tunnels, the children shrieked with delight. Henry, however, had to discipline himself to keep from biting his lips for fear that an oil tanker would choose this minute to ram the tunnel structure.

In Norfolk they took the harbor tour and stayed at a beautiful motel, where the exhausted children were thoughtful enough to collapse promptly into deep sleep, leaving their parents free to experiment with quiet forms of second honeymoon. After that they turned on the free color television. "Will you look at that!" exclaimed Janelle, turning stations rapidly. "Henry, they get the same channels we do in Connecticut. ABC, NBC and CBS. Right here in Virginia." They were both amazed.

"Let's have a long, leisurely breakfast," said Henry the next morning.

Janelle said she would drink to that. They went into the motel restaurant, ordered two highchairs and roped the twins down. The coffee was strong and the cream was real and the matchboxes were worth saving. Unfortunately, Randy began to hit the tray with his utensils and Lindy began to hit Randy with hers and they both tore open a few sugar packets and hurled the contents liberally over their mother, and what with one thing and another, breakfast was neither long nor leisurely and the management seemed quite willing to dump a few hot rolls in a paper bag and send the Davenports on their way.

After that things went steadily downhill. First of all, no one had told them that when the Chesapeake Bay Bridge and Tunnel ended, there was no highway picking it up. They had to wander across the seemingly vacant state of Virginia on tiny ugly two-lane roads that stared at nothing more interesting than old trailers and unpainted shacks and scrubby woods. I-95 was impossibly far away.

"This is like driving through New Jersey," complained Janelle.

"At least New Jersey has a population," said Henry.

"But New Jersey smells," said Janelle.

They agreed not to live in either state and shook on it.

The children, who would celebrate their second birthday in Disney World ("Assuming we ever get there," said Janelle), were atrocious in the manner that only twenty-three-month-old twins can be. They were very small children, having been quite premature and not yet caught up physically, but what they lacked in stature they compensated for in volume.

The Davenports stopped in one dingy little town to buy the children coloring books and crayons and a box of animal crackers. "If we're really lucky," said Henry, "that will entertain them for ten whole minutes." Most of the stores in the village were vacant and most of the people seemed occupied solely with staring at Janelle as she crept into their territory.

They crossed into North Carolina, but nothing changed for the better. The countryside was appallingly empty and dull. "All that's pretty," said Janelle irritably, "is the sky."

The sky, for people who lived under pollution most of the year, was breath-taking. Unfortunately, as Henry pointed out, they could not drive by looking upward.

All of which conspired to make them intensely hungry. They came to Cross Hill, where they would pick up I-95, and stopped at a Hardee's for an early lunch.

The children were asleep in the back seat.

Rule Number One: Never Wake a Sleeping Child.

If they turned off the motor, the kids would be aroused instantly, like wound-up whining machines. But if they left the motor idling, they could zip in, get their orders in a paper bag, slide back into the car, and eat in peace without the clamor of little voices demanding to eat all the French fries and then spilling them on the floor so that no one else could eat them either.

"I love Hardee's," said Janelle as Henry held the door open for her. "The double hamburgers I had at that other one were so hot and the sauce was so tasty and the French fries were so crunchy and the mini pies were so sugary and—"

Henry laughed. "You think they have a hidden camera somewhere, Janelle? Think they'll give you a free lunch in exchange for a testimonial?"

But all they got were two tokens for a machine with googly eyes that spewed out two plastic rings with monster faces.

Henry paid and Janelle, carrying the bag while he carried the drinks, pushed the door open. It was a physical shock to leave the icy draft of the air conditioning for the stupefying heat rising off the asphalt. Janelle steadied herself on the doorjamb. She had truly thought October would be cool. And they had only gotten as far south as North Carolina. For the first time Janelle thought of Disney World in terms of possible discomfort rather than pleasure. Just how hot was it going to be, anyway? Autumn hadn't even come here yet. The leaves had barely begun to turn. If you could call it turning. No orange, scarlet or yellow. Just muddy brown. Because they don't have sugar maples, Henry had said. Whatever, thought Janelle. Autumn isn't autumn without colors to match.

She headed for the station wagon, munching a long, golden French fry that had been poking up above the rest.

The station wagon was not there.

For a weed prospector the field was a treasure trove. Susan even found milkweed pods. Smiling to herself, snipping with surgical precision, she worked her way through the field to the top of the gentle rise.

On the other side the field sloped in what might almost be called a steep fashion to the edge of an old tobacco field, now nothing but stubs in the Carolina red clay, to end at the low bank of a river which flowed quietly on down into more pine woods.

A pastoral scene marred only by the presence of three people at the river's edge who were busily engaged in throwing garbage into the water.

"Of all the nerve!" she said aloud, glaring at them. She'd

certainly known that somebody was responsible for the rusty appliances and beer cans that dotted the roadsides, but she could not remember ever seeing anyone willfully litter before. "And that sure is willful," she muttered darkly. These people had actually bagged their garbage in a heavy-duty black plastic bag, the kind tied with a twisty wire. They must have gone miles out of their way just to throw the garbage in this particular spot. She could see their car, a white station wagon, parked on a dirt path that emerged from the woods below.

The bag did not want to sink.

Susan was too disoriented to be sure, but she guessed the river was Nearing River. Probably too shallow at the edge to cover the bag, she thought. Serves them right. That's disgusting.

She shifted her weed load.

I ought to go down there and lecture them. Ask them what kind of citizens they are, anyway.

But it's perfectly obvious what kind of citizens they are. Not my kind.

She was too far away to guess their sex, but there were two adults in blue jeans and short-sleeved shirts and one tiny child in something green.

One of the adults took a step into the muddy water, retrieved the black plastic bag and threw it again. This time it landed about a third of the way across the river, where a current caught it. The bag wobbled on the surface for a few moments and then it sank. Susan watched the twisty end poke up above the water here and there until the bag vanished.

Go on, she told herself, pick up your feet. Go down there and tell them off.

But they had a white station wagon. People in white station wagons were sinister. Too little imagination to buy in colors. Besides, she could see rust patches over the rear wheel. Never trust a man with a rusty car. Surely somebody had taught her that sometime.

At the river the adults were shaking open another huge bag, getting ready to stuff more garbage in it. That's your cue, Susan, she informed herself. March down this hill and educate those people about litter laws.

But instead she took a few steps backward toward her own car. There was something creepy about this. Every country store had its huge green garbage maw. These people could have flung their garbage away in any of them. Nor did they have to drive off into the middle of nowhere to toss something into Nearing River. Every road for a hundred miles had to cross that peculiar writhing stream someplace.

In the shimmering heat Susan shook her head. The scarf keeping her hair out of her eyes trapped the heat, soaking up the sun like a solar reflector. I have enough weeds, she decided. Probably laws against weed pilfering too. The pot shouldn't run around calling the kettle black.

One of the blue-jeaned people picked up the little child and dropped it in the black plastic bag.

Susan stifled a scream. What are they doing? What a dreadful game! How terrifying for the poor baby! Her hands tightened around the weed collection, cracking the brittle stems, crushing the feathery tips. She waited for the people to pull the child out. To comfort it.

That baby could suffocate in there, she thought, goose-flesh rising on her arms. Don't they know how dangerous it is to have plastic over the face? Don't they know that all dry-cleaning bags should be tied in the middle and then disposed of so children can't reach them?

Susan knew very little about children. One of the tenets of her marriage had been no children. Roger was very firm on that. Susan had agreed absolutely when she was twenty-five, somewhat when she was twenty-nine and not at all now that she was thirty-three. "We have our careers and ourselves," Roger liked to say. At one time that had brought a flush of pride to Susan's cheeks. Now she thought, So what?

The black plastic bag moved as the child inside struggled.

Under the hot autumn sun, Susan began to shiver. Cold-ness prickled its way over her body like some loathsome hand.

The adult who had thrown the first bag tied the top of the second one shut.

She began screaming then. Running down the hill, wav-ing her scissors, Susan listened to a voice that was hers shrieking at a tremendous volume level. A cheerleader's scream, lusty and full, without the slightest edge of fear. She was amazed. In nightmares she never managed to make a sound. Chalk one up for Susan Seton. The weeds caught at her trouser legs and tore her shirt sleeve. There were bram-bles she ran through as if crossing a golf green.

The blue-jeaned adults stared at her. Men. Both of them young men. They looked oddly blank, like photographs on a billboard. "Drop that!" she screamed. "What are you doing? Stop it." Brandishing her scissors, she sped across the tobacco field, raising clouds of red dust.

The men dropped the bag and retreated, exchanging words she could not distinguish, making for their car. She could see rust holes all along the rim of the white station wagon, could see silly purple baubles hanging from the rear-view mirror. The men opened their car door and slid into the front seat.

Susan reached the bag. The child had managed to get partly out. Frantically she scooped it up in her arms.

It was thin and bruised and bloody. Its little clothes were wet with urine and its face was as blank as the men's had been. It stared at her with expressionless eyes and did not move.

The men got out of their car and began to run toward her.

No! Oh my God. Go away. Don't come near me. What is this? Without thought Susan found herself running through the tobacco stubs, back up the slope, carrying the silent, flaccid child. The hill had become Pikes Peak and this time the brambles were winning. She had no breath for screaming now. Hardly enough breath to move. The nightmare was true, after all. When you needed to run, your feet turned to salt pillars.

Behind her the men jogged easily. They were gaining on her.

They were laughing.

The sky was still a soft Carolina-blue. Wisps of cloud drifted across it and a dissolving jet trail arched like a white rainbow overhead. There wasn't any wind except the wind she was making herself. Why are they laughing? Is it a joke?

Will they catch up to me and explain it all and I'll feel like a silly fool?

The laughter was dreadful.

It was evil.

She had crested the slope now; it was downhill all the way to her car. The keys were in her hip pocket. She shifted the silent burden to the other side, ran faster, her free hand scrabbling desperately in her pocket to find the keys. Six keys on the chain. By feel she tried to locate the engine key.

"Hey, lady," shouted one of the men. He dissolved like the jet trail into helpless giggles. Susan hoped it slowed him down. "You dropped your scissors."

She did not think she could get in, throw the child down, slam the door, start the engine and pull away before they caught up. Especially not this engine. Diesels had to wait. What a time to discover a flaw in her wonderful little car. But maybe the engine was still hot. Yes, of course it was, where was her brain, she could crank it right away and—

"Slow down, baby. You're getting all out of breath. We're going to catch you anyway."

He said it definitively. Like an oracle in a tragedy. It was a fact. Susan was crying, she wanted to blow her nose. She could see herself calling "Time!" as if they were all playing a childhood game, setting everything down while the men froze in place so she could find a Kleenex.

She reached the tractor trail and raced the last few steps to her car, ripping open the driver's door. She tossed the child into the passenger side—it seemed late in the day to worry about bruising it—and shoved the key into the ignition.

It was the wrong key.

Sobbing, Susan jerked back the key ring and felt for the right one. House. Office. Trunk.

Car key. She stabbed it in the ignition, turned it, and the side door opened and one of the men got in. He actually sat on the child.

The engine caught. Susan stared at the key, at the glowing red dashboard lights. They are in my car, she thought, and her spine seemed to curve in horror.

"Hey, look, man, she's got doughnuts," he said happily. He took the white bag from the seat next to her and ate one.

She had to force her neck muscles to relax in order to turn her head and look. She dragged her eyes from the car to the men who had laughed, enjoying the chase.

They were young. Perhaps twenty. Unshaven, with long dark unwashed hair and fair skins. One of them would be good-looking if he didn't have acne, laced and torn by myriad tiny scratches. Dots of blood and acne pustules crept over his cheeks. He looked back at her with passing interest, as a dog might, considering whether or not to nip her heels.

Her hand had been rummaging by itself in her purse, searching for Kleenex. Susan stared at the tissue without recognition. The car burbled to itself, with the distinctive metallic idle of diesels. There was no point in driving away when one of them was in the car, eating her doughnuts, stroking her scissors. The other man, leaning in, examining her through the passenger door, held a shotgun. "Glad you came along," he said to her. He spoke without moving his lips. "We needed another car. That wagon was lousy. Yours is nice. What is it, anyway?"

Her jaw had been hanging open like a hungry fish's. She shut it, but it fell back immediately.

"Out of my way, pal," said the shotgun one to the boy with her doughnuts. He moved the front seat forward and slid into the back, taking the bag of doughnuts from his buddy, getting grease on the upholstery where the gun brushed across it. In some way that was both a taste and smell sensation, sour and stale in her mouth, she knew that there would be no explanation because they had no reasons. "Volkswagen Rabbit," she said. "Diesel." She was startled to hear her voice, as calm as if she were arranging a dental appointment. The child had fallen to the floor when the seat was moved. She tried to guess how old it was. Three years? Four? Or perhaps only a year and a half?

At least it was alive. But there was something very wrong about its silence. It should be screaming with terror, not lying there crookedly. I ought to pick it up, thought Susan, tend to its bruises, cuddle it.

But she could not move. Shock was holding her like a strait jacket.

"So start driving, baby," said the shotgun one. "We're going shopping." He fondled the gun as if it were his pet, the beloved dog he had cherished lo these many years.

It was then that Susan remembered the first plastic bag. What had they thrown into the river?

Two

ROGER Seton sold computers. He knew very little about them, but his customers knew less, and Roger was a salesman, not an expert. He had successfully sold greeting cards at age eleven, the only one in the whole elementary school who actually earned money from answering an ad on the back of a comic book. He'd done stints at vacuum cleaners, farm implements, encyclopedias and real estate, but computers suited his life style.

First of all it gave him tremendous freedom. He had all of eastern North and South Carolina for his territory. Susan was used to his being gone several nights a week. Never questioned him. All she asked was a note on the refrigerator giving her an idea of his destination and probable time of return. She hardly ever called him at the motel he chose, which was just as well, because if he could arrange it, he usually had female company.

For Roger Seton, the cardinal rule was always answer the

phone yourself. He prided himself on his juggling of women.

Then, too, he liked computers because he sounded so efficient and twenty-first-century talking about them. Bytes and discs and data storage. He could always impress the relatively small businessmen with whom he dealt, who were taking a plunge truly extraordinary for their area's level of sophistication. The commissions were good, and when the customers had problems—they always did—he could tell them sadly that really top, energetic, imaginative programmers were very hard to find—which was true—and how he wished he had another name to recommend—which he didn't. He didn't care in the slightest whether the hardware functioned the way he'd promised it would. As long as he got the commission, Roger Seton was happy.

Eventually, of course, he'd backlog enough unsatisfied customers that he'd have to leave computers and go on to something else. But he didn't mind. Variety—in sales and in girls—kept the mind bouncing. Roger Seton liked bounce. He never walked anywhere if he could bound. He never went around an obstruction if he could vault over it. He'd been a Marine and still liked to stride. He felt it added to his efficient appearance. A man in a hurry was a successful man.

Life would be just fine if Susan didn't keep plaguing him about having children. Children were all right in their place —after all, he'd been a child himself once—but their place was not Roger's home. It would be altogether too wearing to consider supporting children. And once you had children, all of a sudden you had other things too, like a mortgage and a wife who no longer brought in an income.

He was on his way to Wilmington. Wilmington was a railroad and shipping town and there were plenty of girls. Roger drove steadily down the two-lane road—eastern North Carolina was dedicated to the narrow-road theory—and thought about where he would find someone to share his hotel room that night.

Detective Yates Wolcott of the Nearing River Police Department merely sighed when he heard about Jerry Sam Hopps. Sometimes his job made him dizzy. The punks slunk by with a repetitive ugliness that made it hard to focus on them. Yates had a very hard time telling one from another. He hated testifying in court. He had a fear of perjuring himself, a fear that his testimony would slip from the punk on trial to some other punk, and then another and yet another, without his being aware of it. The judge and the district attorney would stare at him in disbelief and finally in disgust, and the punk would be let off and Yates would be retired.

Sometimes he thought he'd like to be retired. Because then he wouldn't be dizzy. When he had weekends off he helped his daddy on the farm. Kind of liked farming. Rows of peanuts didn't make a man dizzy.

He had to think of something intelligent to do now that they knew Jerry Sam was loose. The trouble was that Jerry Sam would not be thinking intelligently, so it seemed pointless for Yates to do it.

Besides, Jerry Sam would go to Cross Hill, where he had kin. Then he'd steal a gun. If he had the right kind of relatives—or wrong, depending on your point of view;

Yates tried to remember what his point of view was—he'd get the gun from them.

Then he'd commit another crime. Yates gave Jerry Sam till sunset to commit another crime that would put him back in the Correctional Facility. If he'd had to bet on it (sometimes they did), he'd probably have said noon. But sunset was safe. Jerry Sam would definitely not go to bed without stealing something.

The first thing Yates Wolcott had thought the first time he saw the Correctional Facility was how much it resembled the blurry pockmarked photographs of Nazi concentration camps in his books about World War II. The place even looked gray, like a photo, as if it were too tired for color. The fencing—wire, wire and more wire—was far more chilling than solid walls would have been.

Yates thought that rather than publicize Death Row, society should force juvenile delinquents to sit across the road from the Facility and contemplate spending several years there.

But punks were seldom contemplative.

And the ones who left, either by escape (very few) or by parole, never seemed to remember that committing another crime would just put them back. It was fascinating, really. What *were* they thinking about? Somewhere somebody was probably doing a doctoral thesis on it. But Yates would never read it. He only read about the Second World War. He was working on a Herman Wouk novel now. He sighed. Jerry Sam, regrettably, came first.

He went down the hall to the Coke machine. If he threw

enough fizz into his system, the dizziness went away. For a while.

The girl had hair redder than a setter dog's. Instead of tying her hair scarf under her chin, like his mother did to cover up her curlers and rollers, the girl had it tied behind her head, so the red hair kind of poured out the back.

She's got a nice little car, Powell thought, patting the corduroy seat. Got a beagle puppy I'm going to train me has fur soft as this.

He patted the girl's hair, too. It was thick and curly and when he pressed down it squished like a sponge. She gave a lot of funny little shakes, and he thought, She's scared. Like my puppy. Hide under the bed if she could. "Lemme sit in front, Jerry Sam," he said. It would be more fun to watch her face than her shoulders.

"No. We sit in back, so nobody don't see us."

Powell shrugged. "So what kind of mileage you get?" he asked the girl.

Susan Seton was having an extremely hard time driving. She could not seem to remember which foot worked the clutch and which worked the brake. Her stomach was roiling so badly she had to swallow constantly to keep from throwing up. Her eyes darted back and forth between the road, which was no longer a peaceful strip of warm friendly asphalt but a living enemy over which she could just barely steer, and the rear-view mirror, which should be reflecting cars coming up behind her but which was full of leering faces and twisting bodies.

The acned one had been sure the whole world was looking for them. Susan prayed that he was not a wishful-thinking megalomaniac. Probably if she had been tuned to her local radio station, she would have found out that two crazy men in a white station wagon were on the loose. She had thought she was so smart, taking a whole day off in which to daydream and worry about nothing—and look where it had gotten her.

Let the whole world be looking for them, she prayed, gripping the wheel with her damp palms. They passed over the highway she had come off and headed toward FOOD GAS.

People, she thought. Police. Rescue. Helicopter, radios, Canadian Mounties. That's what FOOD GAS means.

He had asked her a question. She had to give an answer. She tried to remember the question. It swirled back out of her memory like the vibrating narration of a science-fiction film. Mileage. "We get around forty-six or seven miles to the gallon," she said. The voice that materialized out of her lungs was calm and level. Perhaps she had turned into an electronic organ and could mechanically choose her volume: This model features the entire realm of sound from soft and sweet to piercing scream. We offer you a special price today because the organ is on the verge of a breakdown.

What are you? A punchy disc jockey? You have been kidnapped, for heaven's sake, stop those crazy inner jokes and think clearly, Susan commanded herself. She did not feel kidnapped. That was a word for ropes around the wrists, chloroform on a damp cloth, whispered phone calls about ransoms, FBI men sneaking among bushes. All Susan felt was fear. Crawling, prickling fear that swept over her flesh in horrid constant waves.

Powell and Jerry Sam had taken their shoes off to be comfortable and Jerry Sam had stuck his bare feet out the front right window to enjoy the wind on his toes. Powell kept adjusting the sun roof to try to get the precisely right amount of sunlight and breeze.

She was an object to them. A driver of a car. They owned her. Like a dog that knew how to heel and would come when called.

The child was still on the floor, folded up awkwardly and staring vacantly at the stick shift. It's concussed, thought Susan, they struck it, I can see the swelling.

She wanted to put it in a more comfortable position. She had a car blanket in the back under the folding section. She wanted to wrap the child up. She could not bear to see it slumped over like a rag doll bent at the wrong places.

But she was afraid to mention it. As far as she could tell, they had forgotten the child. And if they had injured it once, wouldn't they do it again? Better to keep silent.

Criminals kidnapped heiresses or the infants of famous personages. Who was this baby? There was no one famous in Nearing River. And what famous person would be driving a rusted-out white station wagon? But the baby hadn't necessarily come part and parcel with the wagon.

She knew that they had stolen the white car. They were babbling to themselves in the back seat, mostly complaining about the lack of leg room, but also reminiscing over the recent past as if they were two old Navy men getting together for a boozy reunion. "And then remember what happened next?" "Sure I do. That was neat, pal." "Yeah, it was, it was really neat." Laughter.

Outside the window she saw a clump of dried berries that

would look lovely in her vase. She thought about her vase. The vase made her think about her mother, and that made tears prick her eyes. Mother lived in Greensboro, a good four-hour drive to the west. It seemed like a good place to be. Much better than Rose of Sharon Church Slope Road.

Two miles past the highway, but not yet close to FOOD GAS, they came to a grade crossing, and next to it, Rose of Sharon Original Primitive Baptist Church. She looked eagerly at the church, hoping for Circle meetings or Scout leaders' planning sessions. But not one car was parked there. Not a single human being, original, primitive or otherwise.

Susan was so busy examining the church grounds she barely registered the whistle of an approaching freight train. There were no gates to drop down and block passage over the tracks; nothing more than tired peeling white cross signs marked the tracks. The railroad was raised several feet to get above the low and often very wet countryside.

The whistle screamed again, and this time it seemed to be part of her own terror, torn out of her flesh to beg the world to help her. She braked desperately, realizing the danger, slamming her foot much too hard, and the two men in the back were thrown against the front seats.

"Hey. Don't stop," said the acned one. "Step on the gas. You have time, you can beat the train."

Susan looked dubiously down the track. The train had two engines and was whipping toward them. She was not a decisive driver at the best of times. She was the kind who haunted busy intersections afraid to burst out into traffic. She stared at the oncoming engines and was unable to make herself touch the accelerator. "The train is coming awfully fast," she said. Her voice was a cross between a whimper and a scream. She wondered what label it would have on the electronic organ.

"Guess you're right," he said, disappointed. "We'll have to stop. Shoot."

"At what, Jerry Sam?" said the younger one. Abruptly he was very excited, bouncing up and down like a jack-in-the-box. "At what?"

"Not shoot at," said the acned one. "Just shoot. You know, pal. Like dammit. Shoot."

Jerry Sam. So that was his name. Susan bet it was, too. Not Gerald Samuel. Just Jerry Sam.

His pal was completely blank. "Huh?" he said. "Shoot? Dammit?"

"Forget it, pal, just shut up," said Jerry Sam.

He called his friend pal, but in a voice so ugly that Susan shivered whenever the sound emerged. He had a flat motionless face; the words seemed to come out of his pores, because his mouth never moved. The pores flattened out the sounds, made them cruel and long.

There was an engineer at the controls of the freight train. Susan had grown up in a railroad town, she knew the rules. Twice as much crew as could ever be necessary, went the town joke. She would signal them, she would show them what was wrong. No. She would just leap out of the car and—

Dummy, she said to herself. Train's going sixty miles an hour if it's going an inch. What are you going to do? Vault onto an empty flat-bed car?

The engineer grinned down at her and waved. The usual

relaxed, happy grin of a man enjoying every minute of his job. Forlornly Susan looked back at him. But Jerry Sam's pal poked himself up through the sun roof of the Rabbit and eagerly waved at all the train crew. "Hi!" he yelled enthusiastically.

"Will you sit down, pal?" said Jerry Sam.

It was a long, long train, carrying pulpwood stacked in neat cords, going to the paper mills. Sometimes on these trains the pulpwood was stacked badly and the wood began to shift and to fall off, which meant the train had to stop while the crew adjusted the load. Since it wasn't their wood, the crew usually just heaved it over the side, that being easier than restacking. But whatever. It meant time. Time while the train was stopped, blocking the grade crossing.

Have an accident, please have an accident, thought Susan.

"Pow—well!" yelled Jerry Sam. "I said sit down."

His name wasn't pal. It was Powell. Jerry Sam's thick accent, elongated even more by his strange frozen mouth, had tortured the word until Susan hadn't heard it correctly at all. At least now she knew who she was up against. Jerry Sam and Powell.

Powell plopped back down again. "This seat's awfully small," he complained. "How come this back seat ain't any bigger than this, Jerry Sam?"

"Because the Germans didn't build it that way."

"Germans?"

"This here's a Volkswagen. Germans built it."

If anything, the train was accelerating. Despairing, Susan looked out her left window at the church. Surely someone was there. The janitor. The preacher working on his sermons. The church had lovely stained-glass windows with a peculiar bulging look to them. Susan frowned, rubbing her eyes, trying to clear her vision.

There were heavy safety-plate windows over the original stained glass, that's what caused the distortion, she realized. Vandals way out here in the country? Why, that's terrible. Who would—

"Train's gone by, sister," said Jerry Sam. "Why dontcha try driving again?" He rubbed the muzzle of the shotgun over her face. Gripping the golden hoop of her earring, he pulled her head around to face him. Susan's mouth opened in fear and pain—the pierced earring was being pulled viciously—and Jerry Sam shoved the gun right in, pinning her lips to her teeth.

"Man, that's neat," said Powell. "She's really scared now. You really know how to scare 'em, Jerry Sam."

Jerry Sam shrugged. A man who was accustomed to such praise. He put the shotgun down on the floor and told Susan reassuringly, "Next time I'll shoot your mouth off."

Powell roared with laughter. "Hey, that's funny. That's sure funny, that's funny."

"Shut up, Powell."

Susan put the car in first gear. Tears had welled up in her eyes so fast they'd gotten on her eyelashes, and now her sticky mascara made it hard to blink. She struggled to see the road, to choke back the sobs and hide her fear. She had a conviction that it would be wrong to show fear. She must be cool. Blasé even. She filled her lungs with a shuddering heave, throwing all her energy into control.

"Hey. Look down there, man," said Powell. "Bunch of

stray cats. See 'em down by there, at the tracks? Let's shoot 'em. What we got in that gun? Buckshot? Buckshot?"

"Right," said Jerry Sam. "It should really do a job. Spray those cats to hell and gone."

Two cars drove placidly around them, not honking, not even looking. No Southerner objected to a compatriot taking his time on the road. It was one of the privileges of the South.

Jerry Sam leaned way out the right-hand window, aimed the gun and fired on the cats. Susan stared at him in horror. Poor cats, she thought, just scrounging for a living. He has no right to kill them. They've had tough enough lives. Probably a litter of kittens that some mean person dumped here.

She could not watch. She turned her head away, and as the gun went off she was looking at the silent baby on the floor of her car. I forgot you, she thought. I forgot you completely. I was going to try to get out of this car and onto that train and just leave you here. Where is my soul? I've been with these horrid men fifteen minutes and already I am less of a person for it.

"Drive," said Jerry Sam, falling back into the rear. Powell's jabbering pride in Jerry Sam's wonderful aim was like an endless putt-putt motor idling next to her. She could not bring herself to think about what they had done to the cats. She kept her eyes rigidly averted so she wouldn't see in the ditch, but her eyes kept trying to swivel. They wanted to see. Wanted to confirm. The eyes won. For a moment they rested on the shuddering pile of meat that had been the cats.

No. Drive. Just drive. Don't think. But she had some huge source of energy suddenly: physical energy that jerked at her joints. Fear making me twitch, she thought. I have to sit here under the wheel. I can't run. I can't scream. I can't lie down and beat my heels on the cement. All I can do is drive.

FOOD GAS here I come. Just somebody be there. Just see me and do something, that's all I ask. Please, somebody get me out of this.

Three

L AURA JAMES came back from the hairdresser's feeling good. No matter what kind of week she'd had, she could solve her problems under the dryer. A woman could handle anything if her hair was okay. Besides, Laura read confessions while she sat under the hot noisy air that solidified her curls. Whenever you read confessions you always felt reassured that there was a world out there whose problems were a hundred times worse than yours. At least your neighbor's husband wasn't seducing your eleven-year-old daughter.

Timmy wanted to quit high school. Laura and C.D. had screamed at him until their throats and nerves were raw. Timmy kept going on and on about how school was meaningless and he wanted to go out and find himself and get rid of the burden of pointless reports and quizzes, and C.D. kept shrieking that *he*, C.D., might have been dumb enough to quit high school, but no son of his was going to make the same mistake and Timmy was going to school for that diploma if it meant hogtying him to his desk, and if C.D. had to get his belt and take it to Timmy, he would.

Mealtimes had become hours to dread. They would stab viciously at the chicken and chew fiercely on the greens. They would either sit in steaming silence or yell while the food got cold.

Laura patted her hair. The color was pale amber, the wave soft ripples, layer upon layer, until her hair soared in gentle puffs all around her tiny delicate face. Sometimes she just stood in front of her mirror, admiring her hair. She hardly ever glanced at her face, which was ordinary and did not respond to makeup.

She did not know what else to do or say that they hadn't already tried with Timmy. Timmy was seventeen. You couldn't just order him around the way they had when he was little. C.D. had to keep from flying off the handle the way he was. It only pushed Timmy farther out the door. Last night Timmy had talked about California, speaking in a low hypnotized voice about sun and sand and surf and freedom. To Laura, who had never been farther west than Winston-Salem, it smacked of another world, into which Timmy would vanish like a burned-out lightbulb. California seemed to her to be carnivorous. If her son went there, he would be gone forever.

She turned in the drive. Every time she saw her house she felt good; it was a tonic on par with having her hair done. The geraniums in pots by the kitchen step. The gauzy effect at each window where the curtains hung so neatly. And inside, everything just right at last. C.D. had even put up the chair rail she wanted so much to finish off the Williamsburg look everyone had now. And for their anniversary they'd gone to Williamsburg to get the flower prints for the living-room wall and another piece of pewter.

It all matched now. For every object Laura had, she had a matching one evenly spaced from it. She had never been in a house as satisfying as hers.

Her eyes no longer registered the sagging hulk of the old home place behind the ranch house. They hadn't torn it down because tearing it down would take effort and money and also because it was the old home place. You didn't raze your grandfather's house. You just let it slide into oblivion.

Laura parked on the grass near the door. Opening it, releasing herself from the box of controlled atmosphere, she could smell the heavy humid odor of the farm in autumn, a faint fragrance of tobacco that would hang on for months.

She frowned. Zipper wasn't jumping up to greet her. What was the matter with the dog? Timmy had put out fresh water and food before he'd left to catch the schoolbus, she remembered clearly. Zipper couldn't be sick. She'd played with him just that morning.

She walked casually across the yard to the dog run.

The Jameses were a family of hunters. They kept their beagles over at her brother's down the road because they tormented Zipper. But not the way somebody had tormented him now. Laura froze. Accustomed as she was to flesh torn by bullets, the shock of seeing her own beloved Zipper lying in bloody shreds, the flies crawling over his guts, was enough to make her gag.

He was still alive. She gritted her teeth. Somebody would pay for this.

The first thing she had to do was put poor Zipper out of

his agony. She turned toward the house for a gun and saw a broken window over the kitchen sink. The red and gold pattern of the curtain blew through the gaping hole in the glass. A flowerpot was tipped slightly through the same hole.

Laura ceased to breathe.

For a small eternity she assessed the situation. Very calmly she walked back to her car, started it up, reversed out of her driveway and went down the road to her brother's.

"Clothes?" said Janelle Davenport, trembling in the heat. "Clothes?"

"Yes, ma'am, what the twins were wearing."

The officer who questioned her was thick, stolid, with a flat-top haircut. She had not seen hair like that since the last time she glanced at Henry's high school yearbook. Sandy bristles sprouted from the man's scalp like Velcro waiting to be adhered. The policeman frightened Janelle. His very existence implied unknown horrors. The children would be in the car. No one needed to know what they were wearing. No one could have stolen their old beat-up wreck of a car. It had rolled down the hill. What hill? There are no hills in North Carolina.

"Randy was wearing green denim trousers," said Henry faintly. He had changed the children's diapers somewhere in Virginia. Surely he knew what they'd had on. But he was blank. What kind of parents would these police think he and Janelle were? Left their children alone in cars in strange towns. Didn't even know what those children had on.

"And a red and blue polka-dotted shirt," said Janelle. "The clothes didn't match, but Randy loved the shirt, he wore it all the time." The sentence hit her ears like cold water at the beach. She said it all over again, putting the verbs in the present tense. "Randy likes the shirt," she said loudly. "He wears it all the time."

Henry had the little googly-eyed monster rings in his hand. He fondled the plastic, becoming intimately acquainted with every ridge, every imperfection. "Sneakers," he said. "They each had red sneakers with white laces."

"Thank you, sir."

They all said sir. He had never known such polite people. You don't have to be courteous, thought Henry, squinting against the sun. Just find my babies. Stop talking. Let's have some action.

"And the little girl? What was she wearing?"

"The same kind of trousers, I think," said Janelle. "Green denim. But she had a white cotton blouse with puff sleeves and lace ribbon going down the front and a green ribbon in her hair." It had looked festive. Birthday-party-type clothes. Even though Lindy had spilled her cereal over the lace and smudged soggy animal cracker in her hair.

"They're pretty children," said Janelle. No one would hurt a pretty little girl and boy. Whoever stole the car would just get another one. She knew that. She was sure of that. "What are you going to do?" she asked the officer.

"Take you to headquarters to wait there," he said. "It's air-conditioned. You'll be more comfortable."

She didn't care about her comfort. She didn't want to go to the police station. She wanted to stand in the middle of the street and scream their names, make them come running back to her.

Don't panic, she said to herself, don't come apart. They can handle this, they know what they're doing.

Henry gripped the edge of his seat and stared out the window at the storefronts going by. I wonder if they know what they're doing? He thought of Bridgeport and whether it would be better to be having this happen there. It was a peculiar thought. All his thoughts were peculiar right now. He was yearning to be back in the dingy half-occupied town in Virginia, buying animal crackers and crayons. He would have eaten some crackers himself. He wouldn't have gotten hungry so early. He wouldn't have suggested hamburgers to Janelle. It was all his fault; why hadn't he been willing to scoop up the children and take them in? What on earth had made him so unwilling to tolerate a little whining? Randy and Lindy hardly ever fussed; they were good babies.

Henry's breath came in short shallow jerks.

A policewoman led Henry and Janelle to chairs in an unused office. The chairs were heavy dark wood, pockmarked with carvings of initials and graffiti. They looked as if they had been stolen from a high school twenty years ago. *C.F. loves B.D. Mary and Pete were here. Rob loves Bob.* Where? Right here in this chair?

Janelle paced, unable to sit. She was doing so little for her children as it was; it would be the ultimate neglect to sit down. She read the carvings. I love Lindy and Randy, she thought. Tears blotted away everything else.

"I didn't work with him much," said the prison psychologist. He was a young man, with a very young beard, who came one day a week. The SBI officer talking to him could not tell if it was his day for Good Works or if prison duty was some sort of penance. "Frankly," said the psychologist. He waited so long that the officer saw that being frank was definitely not what the psychologist wanted to be right now. "Frankly, I was afraid of him."

Jerry Sam had had the unspectacular hobby of holding up gas stations. He was not the most attractive soul ever kept at the Correctional Facility (few were), but he was not on a par with the rapists, arsonists and murderers either. The State Bureau of Investigation, in the person of Bram Millison, failed to see why a psychologist who worked with the real baddies would find Jerry Sam Hopps a figure of fear.

"Why?" said Bram.

"I guess because he was so detached. There was no point. He had nothing to work with."

"You mean he was retarded?"

"No. No. Perfectly intelligent. Just . . . vacant. None of the . . . the virtues."

Stupid-ass remark, thought Bram Millison. Nobody here has any virtues. How old is this dumb psychologist, anyway? He reeks of college.

"I mean that he lacked any humanity," said the young man. "No interest in people. No decency. No compassion. He reminded me of a robot. Going through the motions of human life."

They're all like that, thought Bram. This kid has a lot to learn. Maybe by the time he has a real beard, he'll have some real sense.

But Bram doubted it.

· · ·

"Tobacco just didn't bring a good price this year," said C.D. James.

The John Deere salesman watched him jockeying for the proper approach. First trying out meek and frightened. Now moving into aggressive and bold.

"I know, C.D.," said Arthur, moving into compassionate but firm, "and I'd like to make an exception for you. But those payments are due. And that's that."

They both knew that was a lie. Exceptions were made all the time. The agribusiness didn't have a whole lot of choice. They couldn't get blood out of a stone and C.D. couldn't make the payments this season and *that* was that.

Arthur swiveled in his chair and tried without success to look tough and authoritative. It was his father's business and he was just filling in temporarily. Arthur was not made for this kind of thing. Farming bored him. C.D. bored him. Even commissions bored him.

The phone rang and Arthur picked it up gratefully. However, it was for C.D. Arthur handed it over ungraciously. He had wanted that call to be his diversion, not C.D. James's.

"Harry?" said C.D., looking puzzled. "Why are you calling me here? Something wrong?"

This is an act if I ever saw one, thought Arthur. Trying to arouse my finer feelings. Tell you something, C.D. When it comes to tractors, I don't have any fine feelings.

"Timmy?" said C.D. "Timmy's hurt?"

Definitely an act. Look at him go all white and tighten his fingers around the receiver.

"You what?" bellowed C.D. "You're calling the sheriff?"

From all over the building, people materialized to find out

why the sheriff was being called and for whom.

"Hey, Harry!" yelled C.D. "Don't hang up. Tell me what's going on."

Arthur could hear the deadness on the line. Harry had hung up. Arthur decided he liked this phone call, after all. It promised to be rather diverting. "What's going on?" he asked interestedly.

"Don't know."

"Why is Harry calling the sheriff?"

"Don't know." C.D. picked up his cap and wheeled around, elbowing past the sightseers.

"What about your payment?" said Arthur. But C.D. was already out the door. Arthur made a face. He was going to have another failure for this morning for his father to jot down. Look at the bright side. Maybe his father would never ask him back again.

"You know, forty-six miles to the gallon is fantastic," said Powell. "I bet that lousy station wagon didn't get fifteen. How many gallons this tank hold, anyway?"

Susan had not the remotest idea how many gallons it held. She gathered the remaining particles of her intelligence and tried to do mental arithmetic. She knew what an average fill-up cost. She knew the price per gallon of diesel fuel. All she had to do, therefore, was to divide—

Divide, thought Susan hopelessly. I can hardly focus my eyes and he's asking me to do long division in my head. "Ten," she said. Ten was a nice safe round number. She could think of lots of things that came in tens that she'd like to have. Ten strong men, ten cops, ten cavalry, ten CB radios to leave on so every trucker in North Carolina could tune in on these conversations.

"Man, we could go five hundred miles in this baby without filling her up," said Powell enthusiastically. "Hey, Jerry Sam. Where do you want to go? Huh? Where do you want to go?"

Powell repeated everything he said until Susan's ears felt assaulted. He was like a child in a self-made echo chamber. First he'd say everything out loud two or three times; then he'd whisper it to himself, savoring it. If he'd been a duck, she would have given him stale bread. Here, duck, duck, duck, duck, duck, duck, duck.

"I haven't decided yet," said Jerry Sam. "Me, mostly I'm just starving."

"Starving, starving," agreed Powell. "Starving."

"Shut up," said Jerry Sam. "What's your name, baby?" He pulled in his feet and leaned over the backrest of Susan's seat to lick the back of her neck.

"Susan," she said faintly. He was the one with acne. She could feel his pimples against her ear lobes. His tongue explored the large round hoop of her earring. Don't pull it again, it hurts enough now, please don't jerk it again. He bit it. Susan gasped, fear loosening her muscles until she was close to wetting her pants. In revulsion she tightened her thighs, forcing herself to stop. The warm wetness between her legs and the saliva spots on her neck brought her to the brink of a scream. She swallowed it.

The baby. Even if I don't keep calm for myself, I have to keep calm for the baby. That's someone's child down on the floor.

The baby's little shirt had a footprint across it, where Powell had rested his shoe. She supposed they could be thankful it wasn't sufficiently alive to cry, or the men would hit it again to shut it up. What was in the other black—

I won't think about that. I won't.

"Susan baby, drive us back to civilization." Jerry Sam took her purse and rifled through it. What he couldn't use he held up through the sun roof and let the wind whisk away. "Seventeen dollars. A Belk department store credit card. A Shell credit card. A BankAmerica charge. I like that, Susan old girl. We can go places on that."

"Won't even be against the law," snickered Powell. "She can sign it herself. Herself. Herself."

"Shut up, Powell," said Jerry Sam.

Susan put an index finger exploringly over the hole where the gold went through her ear lobe. No blood. It only felt torn. She had had her ears pierced last spring. It had seemed like a good idea at the time.

Traffic kept going by in the opposite direction. It was past credence to Susan that no one noticed that anything was amiss. She must look like a perfectly ordinary woman driving two perfectly ordinary men around.

Jerry Sam threw her comb and compact out the window. Then a handful of papers. Susan had no idea what they were. In the face of everything else, it hardly mattered. But her mind made a list, trying to check off what was flying out. Shopping lists? Tax-deductible receipts? Dry-cleaner's tickets? Did she even have anything at the dry cleaner's? Who cares? she screamed at herself. You have a road and two maniacs to cope with. And you're wasting time worrying if you can get back a jacket at the dry cleaner's?

"What's this?" said Jerry Sam. He opened a little yellow plastic cylinder. Susan flinched. "Tampax," said Jerry Sam. He pulled apart the tampon, examining it with great interest. Then he threw it out the window too. "You don't need that, baby," he told Susan, pulling on her earrings. "Powell and I, we're gonna put something else between your legs when we get in the mood."

"Something else," agreed Powell, "something else, something else." He and Jerry Sam laughed insanely.

Susan wet her dry lips. I won't think about that. Look up there. A hawk circling in the sky. Susan chewed on the inside of her cheek. I won't cry. I won't have an accident. With the car or myself.

The hawk was descending now in wide purposeful swoops. It dropped quickly, disappearing from Susan's sight. Snatched up a mouse, she thought; the mouse is caught like me. Claws on its skin.

"I want a hamburger," said Jerry Sam. "Find some golden arches. I need a Big Mac like I have never needed anything before."

Laura James walked slowly through the wreckage of her house. C.D. kept patting her shoulder. "We got insurance," he said weakly. "That'll cover it, I'll call the agent right now, don't you worry, honey, everything'll be all right."

Everything would not be all right. Laura was shaking with rage. The trespass of it. How dare some animal come into her home and break her things, smash her treasure, invade her privacy? She hated the intruder.

She stepped over the broken crockery that littered the kitchen floor. A piece of cereal crunched under her foot. Laura hugged herself to keep from screaming. She had watched a TV interview once in which a psychiatrist recommended screaming as a fine release from tension. Laura wondered what they all would do now if she stopped right here in the hallway, opened her mouth, closed her eyes and hollered for fifteen minutes.

Just looking at it all made her feel dirty. She could not even walk into Timmy's room. The strips of posters hanging from the walls were nightmarish. I have to wash this off, she thought, I touched that table where that monster sat down to eat my food, I have to go wash my hands.

Jerry Sam had been in her bathroom, though. He'd been careful to miss the toilet. Yellow stains covered the white tile walls like a modern painting done on the splash-and-splatter theory. He'd used her white monogrammed towels in lieu of toilet paper and squashed the dried-flower arrangement in its pewter vase by the simple method of stomping on it.

Laura James stopped in the door, opened her mouth, closed her eyes and screamed.

Detective Yates Wolcott listened to the captain's description and shuddered. It took a lot to make him shudder. He swallowed down bile, and it had been a long time since that had happened.

He hated missing kids. They all did. Of course, you always found them. Last time the kid was asleep under its parents' bed. They'd located another fishing happily in a creek, having decided that school was a drag, and another one, conversely, was found sitting weeping in an empty school, still waiting after nine hours for its parents to come and pick it up.

But sometimes on the television news at night you saw the grim outlines of other missing-child cases. Where you had to pretend you needed a snack for an excuse to leave the den until the film ended and they moved on to the Middle East.

"They aren't in Cross Hill any more," said the captain. "And Virginia is roadblocked. So they're probably coming here."

Wonderful. Just what Yates wanted to do all day. Think about what Jerry Sam and Powell would do to two two-year-olds. He remembered his kids at two. Demanding, tugging, noisy. The diapers alone would make Jerry Sam throw the kids out on the pavement.

"White Ford station wagon, 1967 model, rusted out at the bottom, Connecticut plates—that's blue and white, looks like Kentucky—number BB 1971," said the captain. "Hopps likes gas stations. Hit one today, and four that we know of before he got caught before. They got roadblocks up on 301, 48 and I-95. But those two probably know the roads. Might be able to wander in without getting on anything major. We figure they're going to be thinking about their stomachs and their gas tank. The Davenports thought they were down to less than an eighth of a tank. The man remembers thinking he needed to fill up before he got on I-95. Keep your eyes on hamburger joints, zip-in markets, self-service gas, anything like that."

That wasn't much of a request. It only covered a million places. Yates could handle that just fine. Going out, he stared at the map of Nearing River County. It was a parallelogram, roughly twenty-six miles east/west and thirty-one north-/south. It adjoined five counties, three of which were even bigger and emptier. Crisscrossed by roads that few cars traveled regularly.

If they knew what they were doing, they could just vanish in the woods to the east. If they were dumb, they'd come into Nearing River or another town or they'd get on one of the highways trying to drive to the anonymity of a distant city.

Yates thought longingly of his Wouk novel. There wouldn't be time for a chapter tonight.

Father Shields was fishing. He stood beneath the shade of a willow oak and stared mindlessly into the water. It would be nicer to be on the Albemarle Sound, of course, but fishing was fine anywhere. He liked fish. They never told you their troubles.

He liked this spot too. The Episcopal church had been given a piece of land way out in the country for recreation. It had a huge shelter in the meadow for picnics and a small summer cottage that had bathrooms and a kitchen and an enormous fireplace. The teenagers loved it. Wiener roasts, marshmallow toasts. They could not do it often enough.

Happily, they weren't here now. Father Shields was alone with the heat and the mosquitoes and the muddy water and —it was to be hoped—the fish.

He'd heard a car go by on the private lane, but it hadn't stopped, for which he thanked the Lord. The Lord had been stingy with small favors lately; perhaps things were looking up. The car had droned on and stopped somewhere upriver, probably more fishermen, with the luck he was running they would catch all the fish up there and leave the beer cans for Father Shields to snag.

He crunched over a pile of sweet-gum balls, shifting position, casting again. Vaguely he heard some shouting around the bend in the river. For a moment it sounded urgent and he listened, but it stopped and he decided no one needed his help and went on with his fishing.

Time ceased. The sun baked away the annoying rheumatism in his back. Early October. Such beauty. You could convert an atheist on a day like this. Just show him the blue sky and the trees and the fish.

He snagged a plastic bag. Sighing, he jerked at the line. The hook would just rip the plastic and in that way become free to latch on to whatever other debris was in the river. But even when the plastic ripped, the hook stayed firmly on the contents. Father reeled it in helplessly. Just what I wanted, he thought, some litterbug's garbage.

Four

T HE trick was not to think about night. As long as the sun was shining, nothing could happen.

She telegraphed urgency and fear with her eyes to each driver going the other direction. There was no response. Most of them appeared to be singing along with their radios or chatting with invisible people in the passenger seat. They had passed FOOD GAS. It was a collection of motels and restaurants at an enormous highway interchange. But no golden arches. They had to go into Nearing River for those.

She concentrated on her turns. Jerry Sam had ordered her not to get on any major roads, so she was having to thread her way toward Nearing River across the myriad narrow numbered roads. She was only somewhat sure of her direction. But they didn't seem to care how long she took. They weren't even watching the road. Just staring up through the sun roof at the sky while Jerry Sam described his escape for Powell.

Jerry Sam was about twenty-three, she thought. And Powell no more than seventeen. A mere child, Susan told herself, I can handle a kid of seventeen.

One of them could hold me down while the other—

She wrenched her mind off it. There was no percentage in thinking about what they could do to her once night fell. Though why she thought they could rape only at night she didn't know. Physiologically there was nothing to prevent a rape in broad daylight.

Immediately she felt a thousand times more vulnerable. Icy fear rippled like sheet lightning across her body. The wind that had cooled her sweaty forehead chilled her bone marrow. If I get any colder my blood will congeal, she thought. Medical records will be set. Eighty-eight degrees outside and thirty-two under my skin.

"Don't this car have a radio?" said Powell.

"Yes," said Susan.

"Well, turn it on, turn it on. Find some C and W, that's what I like," said Jerry Sam.

She switched the radio knob, but between driving and fear she had no skills left for tuning radios. "Stupid," said Jerry Sam. He stretched between the front seats and adjusted the dials himself. Then he turned the volume up until the entire county must be vibrating from the racket. Susan felt wrapped in noise. They were piling one assault after another on her system. She had always thought of herself as small but tough. Now she felt like crystal. If they happened upon the right pitch, she would shatter. Little shards of her would fall on the asphalt. The state police would come and sweep her up.

If only they would. A sheriff's car had gone past, not even glancing at her. Jerry Sam and Powell, giggling and slouched over in the back, had probably not even been visible.

But I can get away from them once we're in town. A place like McDonald's. It'll be packed. High school kids getting lunch. Travelers getting lunch. Everybody in Nearing River getting lunch. There'll be some sort of opportunity. If Jerry Sam could slip away from a Correctional Facility with barbed wire and dogs and guards holding guns, then I guess Susan Seton can slip away from Jerry Sam in the middle of a McDonald's at lunchtime.

But there was the baby. She'd have to take the baby with her. And there was the shotgun. Susan had a quick vision of how the hamburger crowd would look after Jerry Sam, raging, opened fire on everyone. Like hamburger.

Powell and Jerry Sam told each other all over again about the German shepherd they'd shot up and what fun that had been. And the cats, said Powell, the way that buckshot tore them to pieces. That was really neat, Jerry Sam, really neat, neat. Shut up, Powell.

They're gearing themselves up for bigger and better adventures, thought Susan. At whose expense? The plastic bag — No, I won't think about that, I'll think about the road, I'm coming to an intersection, I have to make a decision, which way Nearing River?

Susan glanced at her watch. It was like waiting for Christmas morning. Or more aptly, for your own execution. Every time you looked at that little dial, with its wide-sweeping second hand, you were equally amazed at how little time had gone by and at how rapidly, nevertheless, zero hour was approaching.

Her mind filled with guesses of what zero hour might consist.

"And then," said Jerry Sam, "I pissed all over their bathroom. Hit the walls, the ceiling, the pretty little towels."

Powell laughed until he cried. His giggle walked up the piano keyboard and then fell off with a splat. As if Jerry Sam were choking him to end it.

She was watching the rear-view mirror more than the road now. The pair mesmerized her. Jerry Sam talked like a ventriloquist. As if he'd had plastic surgery to remove wrinkles and the surgeon had stretched the skin so tight that it would rip if he moved it.

The sun beat down upon her. Truly beat upon her. With a strength that was wooden. At every stop sign, when the wind ceased to fill the car, she was struck also by the heat. Thick spongy waves of heat that sapped her.

The baby lay in its trance across the floor.

"I gotta take a leak," said Powell. "I haven't laughed so much in ages. Ages. Not in ages. Ages."

"Shut up, Powell. Pull over, Susan old girl." The words slithered out of the slit of his mouth.

Susan drove the car onto the shoulder. They weren't fifty feet from a trio of mobile homes.

Maybe there's somebody home, she thought. Maybe I can signal them. Maybe they'll see there's something wrong and they'll—

Jerry Sam and Powell both got out the passenger side. The motor was still idling, she could just drive away—if

Jerry Sam would move over another ten inches, she could just drive away. The car didn't have much pickup, but it had enough, her own adrenalin would make up for it, move over a little bit, Jerry Sam, thought Susan urgently, and then thought, How ridiculous, why am I worried that I might run over his foot? If anybody ever had a foot that deserved running over, it's his.

Jerry Sam leaned in the front, a fringe of teeth showing beneath the straight line of his lips, making a mockery of the word smile, and turned off the motor, taking the keys with him.

I could have driven off. I had a chance right there and I didn't take it because Jerry Sam Hopps might have gotten his toes hurt. I had the car and the baby and the shotgun all to myself and I didn't even move. Dope. Idiot. Clod.

She hoped the people in the trailers would call the sheriff about two adult males exposing themselves in public. She hoped that the dogs tied to one of the trailer hitches would break loose and come over and bite off everything that was exposed—that would teach Jerry Sam a thing or two. She hoped—

Stop it, she ordered herself. You're accomplishing nothing.

She slid over and awkwardly pulled the child up off the floor. It was limp but still breathing in a shallow, ragged fashion. She pulled its clothes off, and since they were soaked from ankle to shoulder with urine she threw them out the window. If Jerry Sam could litter, Susan could litter. Litter. Black plastic . . . don't think about that. The baby is a boy, I'll have to stop thinking of him as it, I wonder what his name is. His poor mother.

She got out of the car and went around to the rear. Pressing the silvered key knob she opened the rear window upward, which automatically lifted the lid of the small storage compartment behind the seat. Jerry Sam and Powell watched her silently. She was after the car blanket Roger had bought her once. It was still in its heavy clear plastic sheath because Susan had never had occasion to use it. She could wrap the poor baby boy in it. She had a conviction that anyone sick or hurt should be swaddled and that would relieve half the symptoms right there.

Tools. For repairing flat tires. A tire iron. A long slim heavy black tire iron. Susan's fingers strayed across it.

Could I do that? Could I hit someone hard enough to incapacitate him? My life is at stake and so is this baby's. I need to hit Jerry Sam. I play tennis, I have plenty of arm muscle. One good swipe and I could catch him right across the eyes and that would be that. Powell is the type to run. And these trailers have telephones, even if nobody's at home. I could break a window with the tire iron if the trailers are locked. Or I could just drive away, take the keys from Jerry Sam's limp—

But it was not the tire iron that she picked up. It was the plaid blanket. She was not ready to strike anyone. Not ready. An unexpected choice of words. It implied that later (and what was contained within "later"?) she would be ready. Ready for what? Did she have to primed, like a pump? Was she being revved up for some dreadful violent scene? Susan shivered. She carried the blanket around the car to the child.

They were coming back to the Rabbit, zipping themselves up, laughing loudly. Jerry Sam's laugh crawled out from between his rigid lips like a rat from the sewer.

Gently she folded the fringed ends around the baby. Its color was terrible. I have to say something, she thought. I have to assert myself. Maybe they just don't realize. Maybe all it will take is a calm reminder. "The baby is really quite severely injured," she said to them. "Why don't we leave him on the steps of that trailer? They could take care of him for us. Then he won't be in our way." *Our way.* What am I talking about? This is not a joint enterprise we have going here.

"Susan, I got news for you," said Jerry Sam. "We ain't never been taking care of him." His laugh crawled out again.

She took a deep breath. "You know babies. They cry and whine. Nuisances. It would save us all a lot of trouble to leave him for somebody else to watch."

"Like we left his sister, huh, Powell?" said Jerry Sam. They went into their laughing routine again.

"How did you leave his sister?" whispered Susan. She already knew. She had known standing at the top of the weed field. She had known running back up, clutching the baby in her arms.

"In the water, Susan old girl. Neatly bagged. I am nothing if not neat. Now start the car. You are taking your own sweet time getting us into town and I am sick of it. Step on it."

Pete Williams was a cop. He also worked odd hours at the One Minute Shop across from McDonald's. The only good thing about the One Minute Shop—aside from the pay; you didn't support three kids in braces on a cop's salary, not in

this poky town anyway—was that it was across from Mc-
Donald's. Every time Pete figured he couldn't stand that
stupid store one more One Minute, he'd race across the
four-lane traffic and get himself a hamburger.

"You're eating up all you earn," said his wife in disgust.

At least he was retaining his sanity.

"And what about your waistline?" demanded his wife.

Pete sold a lady a gallon of milk and a loaf of bread. He
gave nineteen dollars and seventy-six cents' change to a kid
who wanted gum. He sold a confession magazine and a bag
of corn chips to a girl on her lunch hour and a six-pack of
beer to some construction guys on their lunch hour. The
usual stimulating array of customers.

"Hot enough for you?"

"Shorely is hot."

"Thank you, ma'am, y'all come back."

"Yes, sir, and cigarettes, please."

"My, that's high, you really charge that much?"

"Y'all come back now."

He had to have another hamburger. It was imperative that
Pete Williams should have another hamburger. It was the
only thing between him and the loony bin. "Jimmy," he
yelled into the back, "I'll be right back, take over for a
minute."

He knew, he could feel it right in his bone marrow, that
the One Minute Shop would get held up sometime when he
was across the street stuffing his face. The rest of the police
force of Nearing River would laugh until it wept.

He got an iced tea with extra ice and a burger. He was

just walking toward the side door when he saw Susan Lonergan coming in the front.

Lord have mercy. How many years had it been since he'd seen Susan Lonergan? She was just as cute as ever, small and slim and still that perky, fluffy red hair sprouting all over the place. Looked a little peaked, though. He wasn't surprised. She'd married that jerk what's-his-name. The one who couldn't stick at anything except girls. Peter wondered if the guy, what *was* his name, had given up his girls for Susan. He hoped so. Susan was a doll. But he doubted it. Roger Seton, that's who it had been. Big, pushy, football-playing, cocksure Roger Seton.

Never could stand that ass, thought Pete Williams. Bet he's still playing the jock.

He walked, grinning, across the floor to greet pretty little Susan Lonergan.

"Now the thing of it is," said Jerry Sam, "that you got to do what I tell you, Susan old girl." He took her scissors from Powell, who'd had them thrust in his jeans pocket, and he stroked her cheek with the blades. He let the points drift right up against her eyelashes and he pressed. She shrank back into the upholstery, whimpering and begging. Jerry Sam grinned back behind his teeth. "You go in and get us our hamburgers. And I'll be holding the kid here. You want me to put this scissors in the kid's eye?"

"No," said Susan. Constant fear was like having the flu. Her entire body was throbbing.

"You don't say nothing to nobody except your order. Got that?"

"Yes."

He took the scissors away and looped a finger through the golden hoop of her earring. "You gonna be good?"

"Good," muttered Powell. "Gonna be good, gonna be good."

"Yes," whispered Susan. Please don't rip my ear, she thought, clenching her fists against the pain, please.

"Call me sir."

"Yes, sir."

He opened the front door for her and Susan got out. Her legs were trembling. At least the wet spot on her trousers had dried in the heat. She walked one step. "Would it be all right if I went to the bathroom?" The words shook on the hot air like exhaust fumes. Thin, ephemeral, lost.

"Sir," corrected Jerry Sam.

"Sir."

"The whole sentence, Susan old girl, and get it right." Powell giggled.

"Would it be all right if I went to the bathroom, sir?"

"Whaddaya think, Powell?" said Jerry Sam.

"Sure. It'll ruin the upholstery if she goes in the car."

They both laughed. "You may go now," said Jerry Sam, mincing the words like a mock English actor.

Susan's feet found the sidewalk and led her to the entrance to McDonald's. The door was impossibly heavy. She strained to move it. Inside, the lunch crowd had gone. The counter girls sagged over the shining ledge, pads in hand.

"Hey, Susan," called someone cheerfully. "How ya doin'?"

She did not recognize the voice. Maybe it was another

Susan the man wanted. Lots of Susans in this wicked world. If it was her, tough tiddlywinks. She couldn't talk. Jerry Sam probably could not see through the darkly tinted glass that wrapped the restaurant, but she couldn't be sure. She couldn't let him blind that poor dying baby. And he would. He wanted to. He had positively blossomed when he shoved the scissors against her own eyes. She had thought his acne would burst from the excitement.

Woodenly Susan walked toward the rest rooms. The voice didn't call again. She shut the compartment door behind her and vomited.

I'm sick. I can't go on with this. I need to take two aspirin and go to bed.

She straightened up with difficulty.

I can't take too long, she thought, suddenly frenzied. They'll get mad. They'll hurt the baby. Stop vomiting. Go to the bathroom. Who knows when you'll get another chance.

Would they make her go by the side of the road? Would they—

She cleaned herself up, pawed at the hairdo that had been completely ruined by the wind and Jerry Sam, adjusting the green scarf, and rushed out to the counter.

She could not remember what Powell had decided on. He had wanted a Dr. Pepper first, and then a Coke and then said no, only Pepsi. Or was it the other way around? What would they do if she brought the wrong drinks? Susan could not breathe. She managed to open her fist. How had she gone to the bathroom without ever opening the hand where the dollar bills were clutched?

"Miss?" said the counter girl. "Take your order?"

Dr. Pepper. She was sure of it. She gave the order.

"Hey, Susan! Good to see you. It's been years."

And what if it wasn't Dr. Pepper?

"Susan? You Junior League these days? Can't talk to the peasantry? It's me—Pete Williams."

She did not look at him. She smiled in the direction of the napkins and salt and paid for the hamburgers and French fries. The girl tucked the order on a gray cardboard tray, neatly fitting the drinks on the little pop-up holes.

I wonder who invented that little tray. It's very clever. Pete and I were in high school together. He helped me break into my locker once when I couldn't get it open and there were papers in it I had to have for French.

Pick up the bag and the tray. Turn. Leave the restaurant.

"Susan? You all right?" Anxious but mad. Don't notice me, Pete, thought Susan. I take that back. Notice me, notice me. But don't let it show. Oh my God, he's following me out the door. Drop dead, Pete Williams, can't you see I have two men in my car looking for an excuse to blind a baby? Don't look, yes, look, look, look, now I sound like Powell, jabbering in my beer, Pete, just trip over a hot dog, why don't you?

She made it to the car. The smell of the grease on the French fries nearly gagged her. I won't vomit. I've already played that scene.

She balanced the cardboard tray gingerly, opened the door and got in. Pete had stopped at the restaurant exit. Out of the edge of her vision she could see him lounging there in the door. Letting all the air conditioning out. The management would love that.

She handed out the food to Jerry Sam and Powell.

"Hey. You could have got something for yourself," said Powell. "It's your money."

"No, thank you," she said, turning the ignition. "I'm just not very hungry." She'd had a sip from the water cooler to take the burn off her throat from the vomiting. The radio came on, its blare filling her ears and nose and sinuses. She reached numbly, blindly, and lowered the volume. The relief was physical.

"Sir," corrected Jerry Sam.

"Sir." Was Pete watching? Could he see something wrong? Would he wonder who the two men were that Susan Lonergan Seton was toting around?

"Whole sentence, Susan old girl."

"I just wasn't very hungry, sir." Or was Pete just put out that Susan was too high and mighty these days to be bothered speaking to an old friend?

"Attagirl. Head for the highway now."

"Ain't we gonna go shopping now?" said Powell, whining.

"You stupid dude, we were gonna shop for a radio. She's *got* a radio." Jerry Sam munched his hamburger contents separately. First the pickle. Then the bits of onion.

Susan drove cautiously around the back of the restaurant to the exit lane. In the rear-view mirror she could see that both men were totally engrossed in their hamburgers. She looked for Pete. She could signal him, mouth HELP, or flash her headlights or—

But he was gone.

She blinked back tears and turned the car around to face the EXIT sign. "Which highway did you want?" she said. "There are several."

The scissor point came so sharply in her back that she screamed, throwing herself against the steering wheel to escape the blades. "Why did you do that?" she sobbed. It hurt terribly. But she couldn't tell if it was real hurt—the kind that bled—or terror. She wanted to take her back off and look at it. Or run inside to her mother for a kiss and a Band-Aid. She hunched over the wheel, weeping.

"Shut up!" hissed Jerry Sam. "Stop your noise. People will look. I gave you an order. If you forget to call me sir one more time, I'm cutting off your earring. That means like ear and all."

Her hands were so wet with perspiration she could hardly hold the wheel. Her left knee had developed a twitch. She watched it between the arms of the steering wheel. It jerked as if a cartoon doctor were hitting it with a hammer. "Which highway, sir?" she whispered.

"I read about that in the paper once," said Jerry Sam to Powell. "Some dude got kidnapped, and to prove they really had him, they cut off his ear and mailed it in to his family."

Powell giggled.

Behind them a car raced its motor.

"Aaaah, hell. Just turn right," said Jerry Sam. "I don't know where I want to go yet."

She jerked out in traffic, the car bucking as if she'd never touched a manual transmission in her life. Second gear crunched. She slid into third, stalled, rammed back into first, the gears raking raspingly. Sobbing, she managed to restart the car and get them going properly. In typical Southern fashion, none of the cars near her honked or even seemed disturbed. They merely waited for the little lady to remember how to drive. A truckdriver passing on her left gave her an amused smile.

"Let's go into the stores anyway," said Powell. "Come on. We got lotsa money. Let's, okay, let's."

"I can't be shopping all over town right after I got myself out of prison," said Jerry Sam irritably. "Got to take some care."

"So send her in for us."

"What do you want to buy so bad?"

"I don't know. I don't care. I just wanna go shopping."

"Shut up, Powell."

She had no Kleenex. Jerry Sam had tossed it all out the window back on Rose of Sharon Church Slope Road. She sniffled powerfully, but it was no use. She had to wipe her nose on her sleeve.

The baby was still curled in its silent huddle.

Where are we going? What's going to happen? The only thing I'm sure about is this baby's life expectancy.

Ahead of her the asphalt blurred. She let the tears roll across her cheeks. The wind coming in the opened windows dried it quickly, leaving white salt trails across her face.

Five

"Just marched into my room, sassy as you please," said Miss Melchior.

The sheriff admired her for a moment. He had had her for a teacher himself several times. Not Miss Melchior in the flesh, of course. But one like her. Stout, straight, firm. People complained these days about kids, about how teaching was another world from what it had been years ago. Sometimes he wondered. He bet Miss Melchior didn't have discipline problems. He bet during the very first week of integration, when the whole school was a hand grenade in the palm of a spastic, that Miss Melchior hadn't had discipline problems. He could just hear her addressing that first black and white class, in a voice that brooked no opposition, "There will be no demonstrations in this room save the demonstration of scholarship. Open your books. Grasp your pencils. We shall commence."

"Melchior?" he said. "That's like the king?" He grasped his pencil and notebook and commenced.

"Precisely."

"What did he do, ma'am?"

"Demanded to have his cousin Powell. Demanded, if you please. I had Jerry Sam Hopps in this very classroom for two years and I flunked him each time. They frown on flunking now, you know. They beg you to take into consideration the deprivation from which the poor little dears sprang. One could hardly dispute the fact that Jerry Sam was deprived. But was it relevant? The objective was American history. I could not relate that to the fact that his father drank."

"No, ma'am. I quite see what you mean." The sheriff loved it. The vocabulary, the intonation, the posture as Miss Melchior stood guarding her desk. It was perfect. High school memory incarnate. "And what was it he did after he entered the classroom demanding Powell?"

"Powell rose to his feet, and I may say that that boy often has trouble achieving even that. A distinctly low creature. Powell was so low that the other students did not even bother to put him in their pecking order. He stuffed his hands in his side pockets, threw his back out of joint in order to effect the desired stance, and sashayed across the room between the desks like the king of the mountain." Miss Melchior sniffed. Clearly she had not been able to see Powell in the role of king of the mountain.

"Yes, ma'am?"

"I said, 'Jerry Sam Hopps, what are you doing in my classroom? You know perfectly well you're supposed to be in prison.'"

The sheriff couldn't contain the laugh that bubbled up in him.

Miss Melchior was affronted. "That," she said huffily, "is precisely how my class reacted. They all laughed. Guffawed would be a more appropriate word. I nearly lost control. Why, it took us as much as three minutes to return to silence after that nasty pair left."

Three minutes, thought the sheriff. Man, she is tough. I can't get silence at my own dinner table in three minutes. Matter of fact, I haven't had silence when I asked for it in years.

"A second-rate silence at that," she added, frowning at the memory. "An undercurrent of chatter prevailed for the remainder of the period."

"Did Hopps give any indication as to where he might be planning to go with Powell?"

"No," said Miss Melchior. "They did not linger."

He thought at first that it was an old doll. He even noticed how lifelike it was and marveled at how wonderful the plastics industry had become—the softness of the vinyl, the limp reality of the pretend hair.

But the arm he held was warm and had blue vein lines and tiny fine golden hairs and even a few freckles.

For a moment Father Shields could not think at all. The recognition that this was a real child was too much for him to absorb. Afterward it seemed to him that he had stood for a major portion of his life poised on the edge of the river, holding by its arm a doll that was a dead child, half in and half out of a black plastic garbage bag.

It was hard to describe to the policeman what had happened next. He knew he had given the child mouth-to-mouth resuscitation, that he had rubbed its little limbs in a hopeless effort to make the blood circulate, that his own tears had interfered with the tasks. Why didn't I ever take a first-aid course at the Red Cross? he chastised himself. What kind of a Christian am I, anyway?

There had been the terrible decision whether he should go on trying to revive the child or drive it into the hospital. He knew enough to know that every second counted. He also knew that he didn't know how to resuscitate anyone. Sixteen long miles no matter how direct a route he took. Desperately he tried to remember which of the little settlements in the county had rescue squads, how to get to them the quickest. The mental map in his mind of the county in which he'd lived for most of his adult life disappeared.

He had wasted precious seconds staring helplessly at the lacy blouse and green pants on the tiny limp girl and then ran with her to his car, which was parked behind the recreation house, hidden by clumps of rhododendron. He almost screamed for help, but he realized fearfully that whoever had done the shouting upriver a few minutes earlier must have been the one to dump the child in the water.

He remembered that he had not prayed. He had not even thought of the Lord. He had thought only of physicians, white-coated, calm, capable, hypodermic-wielding physicians who could save anybody, of course they could, he was sure of it, just drive fast enough and everything would be all right.

He had spent the summer on an exchange plan with a

member of the Anglican church, had lived nine wonderful weeks in a little English village near Oxford. Now he could not recall whether it was England or the United States where you drove on the right. He careened down the road, letting the car have its head, letting the wheels turn where they would.

There were too many cops covering the county searching for the Davenport twins and Jerry Sam and Powell Hopps for Father Shield's erratic driving to go unnoticed for long. He heard the sound of a siren behind him like a call to heaven. He slammed to a stop, barely missing a telephone pole, one wheel in the drainage ditch, and almost fell out of the car with the child. Words came out of him like rain from a spout, but none of them were adequate for the horror he had felt, taking a real child from a garbage bag.

Susan had gone to the mountains once in October, years ago, with a church youth group. She remembered the vivid oranges, golds and reds of the leaves. It had been incredible. Truly. The word meant past all believing. She, Susan Lonergan, had not believed it. Autumn in eastern North Carolina meant a lot of leaves turning brown and falling in the grass that was already brown from the summer's heat.

Pete Williams had been on that trip. She could see him now, jaunty, laughing, silly Pete, leading everyone on the bus in some hundred-verse singsong.

Ahead of her stretched the highway. On the sides, now that they were beyond the city limits, were a lot of trees. Brick houses were scattered among them. One of the trees was ablaze with orange. Her eyes rested on it, for one tiny moment savoring the sole scrap of beauty she'd seen in a day that was lasting a lifetime. The leaves had a peculiar clarity of shape and every tinge and hue of color seemed masterfully done.

On her wedding day, after all those months of preparation and parties and planning and shopping, Susan had stood at the front of the aisle and surveyed the guests and the groom and the flowers, and thought to herself, I don't believe it. This isn't happening.

Here she was—being kidnapped by two deranged amoral men and she had had no preparation whatsoever for the experience, but also she had no trouble believing it. Perhaps it was the smell. The sour pimply odor that—

Peter Williams had become a policeman.

Susan wilted over the wheel and the road in front of her wavered as if it were under water.

I was right there. Safe. Home free. I could have spoken to him out of the corner of my mouth. He would have known what to do. He would have telephoned, would have done something sensible, gotten me and this baby out of this mess. Oh dear Lord. Why didn't I remember that Pete Williams became a cop?

Her bones were softening. They were having a harder and harder time supporting the jelly that her muscles had become. Her fingers were lying asleep across the steering wheel, not even attempting to grip the fake leather that Roger had tied around the wheel for a classy effect. Her eyes were so tired they were crossing. She lost track of the white line in the road.

Sitting here thinking Somebody save me, Susan screamed

at herself. How're they going to save me when I don't tell them something's wrong? Dummy, dummy, dummy. It's too late now. Pete Williams is a cop, but he's two miles away now and—

There was a roadblock ahead of them.

She had never seen a roadblock before except on television. Finally I know why I watch television, Susan thought giddily. So I'll recognize roadblocks and guns when I see them. That group of state police cars up there, that is called a roadblock. It blocks the road, you see.

Jerry Sam and Powell were still lounging in the back, licking the last bits of grease and salt out of their bags of French fries. She wondered if she should mention the roadblock. Or just drive up to it and try to hop out before the scissors or shotgun attacked. Jerry Sam was cradling the gun in his lap. She tried to reason out the proper move, but she seemed to have lost her intelligence. It had grown tired of living in a vacant building and had walked off to find better quarters.

Jerry Sam began cursing, bouncing all over the rear seat, having spotted the roadblock at last, screaming contradictory orders at her. "Turn the goddamn car around, Susan. Go back. No. Go right on through it, we'll bluff our way. No, don't. Turn around, turn around, Susan!"

She changed lanes to get in the left-hand lane prior to swinging a U turn, but there were cars coming the opposite way. Cars the police had let through their roadblock.

"But if she turns around," objected Powell, "the cops will see."

"Better they should see from down there than from any

closer," said Jerry Sam. "Swing the goddamn car around, Susan. Move it!"

He pressed the scissors against her cheek.

See me! she thought at the roadblock. Don't just stand there stopping cars—See me! She tried to make the thought a neon sign that the police would easily read at five hundred yards. Or however far off they were. She was no good at distances.

"Susan. Turn." The scissors pressed deeper into her soft, vulnerable cheek, only an eyelash away from her right eye. She leaned on the horn to warn the utility van coming the opposite way, jerked the wheel hard to the left and swung the car directly into the path of the van.

For a moment her entire existence was a looming, shiny side of navy-blue van, an answering horn that blared into her ears like Judgment Day. She saw a horizontal strip of chrome and a small dent right below it: I'm going to hit him, that dent is my target. She wrenched the wheel.

The driver of the van was shaking his fist, looking equal parts terrified and enraged; like a recipe, thought Susan, cream equal parts butter and sugar. Then frantically he applied both hands to his own wheel and gave her space. She watched the van slide off onto the shoulder to let her in his lane.

She was across the white line, tires screaming, leaving patches of rubber that she would have paused to admire at the tender age of sixteen, desperately straightening the car, hanging on to the wheel as if it were her living savior. The car did not have power steering; it took all her strength to move the wheel. She came within an inch of the van—she knew that much about distances—and then somehow she was facing the right way again and finding another gear.

Jerry Sam and Powell were shrieking like cheerleaders. Powell bounced up and down until his head cracked against the roof of the car. Jerry Sam pounded the floor with the shotgun at the same time that he shoved the scissors in her face. A grammar school child patting his head and rubbing his stomach together. She prayed for his coordinations. If he pounded the scissors and shoved the shotgun, she would be blinded.

She could not figure out why the car was behaving so sluggishly. Diesel compacts had not been designed for zero to eighty acceleration in record time, but they had more pickup than this. The car chugged. She had gone from first into third. No wonder it's staggering, she thought. She down-shifted, floored the accelerator and zoomed ahead; shifted back to third, ripped into fourth. The engine throbbed until its vibrations covered the blare of the radio. The diesel shot ahead; its speed was much greater now than the other cars on the road, who were close enough to state troopers to maintain a meticulous fifty-five. The diesel leaped past its competition. It was like driving on cross-stitch embroidery—X-ing between cars, sliding on a needle.

"Way to go!" yelled Powell, bouncing. "Beautiful."

"Look at 'em," breathed Jerry Sam all over her neck. "Look at 'em move over for us. Go, Susan old girl, step on it."

There was a terrible grinding clanking noise behind them, as of several train cars joining. Susan tried to see in her rear-view mirror what was happening, but all it reflected was Powell's shirt moving up and down like the lines on a broken color TV set.

"Get off the highway," yelled Jerry Sam. "Turn right here. Onto that side road. Turn, Susan, turn."

She wrenched the wheel again, skidding, following his directions with machine-like efficiency. The little car moved like its name. Rabbit-style, jerking left and right, it hopped suddenly when she unintentionally struck the curb.

Part of Susan was highly impressed. Who would have thought that little old phone-answering, typewritering, dental appointment-making Susan Seton could drive like a drag-strip entry?

The rest of her strained to hear sirens. There had been enough police cars down there to start a war. Where were they now? Why weren't they tearing up the pavement to follow her?

"A roadblock," said Powell reverently. "For us. You *do* think it was for us, don't you, Jerry Sam?"

"Course it was for us," said Jerry Sam. "For me, actually. They don't even know about you. I'm the one escaped." He admired his fingernails in the manner of a casually successful man being interviewed on television talk shows.

Susan could not hear sirens. What was taking them so long? They couldn't pretend they hadn't noticed. She had not tiptoed through the tulips.

"Hey, man. We got away," said Powell happily. "We done got away." His giggle jackhammered Susan's skull. "Got away," whispered Powell to himself, "got away, away, away."

Six

"**I** TOLD you," said Elmina Davenport. "Didn't I tell you? Didn't I tell you, Henry?"

Of course she had told him. His mother's life consisted of telling other people the dire things that would befall them if they didn't take her advice.

"I told you you should of spent your money on a nice new car. Or at least some decent furniture instead of that old used stuff you have now. But no. You and that Janelle. All so hot to go to Disney World and have some fun whirling around on mice. I told you what would happen when you drove through those redneck uncivilized places. I told you."

Henry could no longer remember why he had telephoned his mother. There were words in the dictionary like sympathy, love and help. But none of them seemed applicable to Elmina Davenport.

He held the phone away from his ear and let his mother drone on. She was happy. She was happy, for the love of

Christ, because his babies had been kidnapped. By two young punks who might do anything and everything to them. Her own grandchildren. And she was happy because it proved her right.

Janelle lay in the hospital bed on the other side of the telephone table. She looked so young and frail against the white crispness of the sheets and the pale-blue thermal blankets that warded off the chill of the air conditioning. It wasn't an uncivilized redneck place. Everyone had been wonderful, really. The doctor had spoken softly, like a gentleman in a movie starring gentlemanly Southern actors, reassuring, neighborly, not mentioning the hypodermic until it had sunk into Janelle's arm.

"I'd like to give you a tranquilizer too, young man," he said courteously. "But it's not urgent. Your wife was coming apart. And that won't help."

"My seams are fairly strong," said Henry. And they were. He thought now that it must have come from years of listening to Elmina Davenport's predictions. Hardened the soul. Not that his heart felt hard. It felt like old Jell-O. Shaky. Shivery. With a very thin skin of control that the slightest push of a spoon could pierce.

He hung up on his mother.

The cop's name was Martinez. He was not a native. The only names in Nearing River County were Anglo-Saxon and the only shades were white—very white—and black, which could be anything from pale, pale tan to deep chocolate-brown. Any features neither Negroid nor Anglo-Saxon were so foreign as to be traffic stoppers. Martinez had come

to Nearing River by way of New York City and D.C., both
of which he had heartily despised, and rural North Carolina
was another world. Sometimes he felt like a visitor who'd
fallen off a UFO. But his wife was happy (after three years
here she'd actually met another living, breathing Roman
Catholic in the same neighborhood) and the kids had lots of
friends and the living was good. His largest problem was not
laughing when his colleagues, both the very white and the
varied black, muttered darkly about the evils of busing.
They ought to try the evils of urban living, he thought, that
would be a breath of polluted air for them.

The kidnapping of the little Davenport twins had not
shocked him nearly as much as it had the others. But that
didn't mean he wasn't concerned.

He bundled the priest into the back seat, turned on his
siren and his radio and got the word out. It wasn't easy.
Considering the man was a priest and priests made their
living with facile words, this Father Shields was remarkably
inarticulate. It was all Martinez could do to keep from
screaming at him. Finally he decided that screaming was the
best course of action, after all, and he hollered for an end to
the babbling. Shut up or talk helpfully, he commanded, and
the father gulped and talked helpfully.

Martinez gave the location of the recreation house, the
description of the creek edge, mentioned the shouting just
upriver that Father Shields had ignored, stated the times
Father thought all this had happened. As he spoke, he drove
one-handed down the four-lane highway he had reached so
easily and knowledgeably from the mass of identical roads
that had rattled Father Shields so completely.

It was one reason he'd become a cop. He loved speed driving. It was always good to see the traffic parting nervously in front of him, to manipulate his car past the obstacles, to hear the muted shriek of his own siren.

The presence of Lindy Davenport in the back seat detracted considerably from today's pleasure, however. Never had the county seemed so large. In D.C. you couldn't get yourself more than blocks from the nearest emergency room. Of course, in D.C. you'd have to wait six hours once you got there because of all the OD's and knifing victims ahead of you, not to mention the fourteen-year-old mothers busily having their second illegitimate child in the hall.

He concentrated on the road.

Lindy Davenport had started breathing again.

Roger Seton deliberated for quite a while over which hamburger to order. He never tired of hamburgers. It was Susan who was in love with casseroles and salads and eggs. Always puttering around the kitchen, fussing over her cookbooks, polishing her copper bowls. Planning those menus he detested and then getting upset when he declined the hollandaise sauce and reached for the ketchup.

Me, I could have hamburgers for breakfast, lunch and dinner seven days a week, he thought. He decided on a double burger with extra cheese.

The little girl who was serving him was a sassy little number. He frowned. She wasn't much more than sixteen. It seemed to Roger that the girls were getting younger and younger these days.

The girl gave him the required smile, thanked him for

coming, hoped he'd have a good day and come see us. She
was already smiling at another customer before Roger could
get his thank you out.

He shrugged and skipped it. She didn't deserve it anyway.
The French fries weren't as hot as he liked them.

If I weren't married I'd be more attractive, he thought. I
have that married look. Susan's given it to me. I ought to
give up marriage.

It wasn't a new idea. He often toyed with it. He planned
to exit dramatically when he exited. Vanish, maybe. Throw
a real scare into Susan. Shake her out of the stodgy life she
liked so much. Let her see a little reality for a change.

On one bank of the river—it was Nearing River Branch
Creek—was a very old stone mill. Out of use for two
decades, it sat in gray bleakness, its windows gone, X's of
peeling wood nailed from the inside to prevent entrance
through them. Two stories on the land and three over the
water, it had a fine arched sluice gate through which water
poured and a leaking stone dam which formed on one side
a lovely millpond and on the other a swirling array of currents.

A gristmill when built, it had become a factory during the
Civil War for the production of Confederate uniforms.
Since then it had become, according to the whims of its
owners, a sawmill, a cotton-yarn factory, and once more a
gristmill. It was in the local historical association's register,
but the only signs on it of any interest were the ones that
said NO TRESPASSING.

The twisting mass of currents caused by the dam spills

and the sluiceway and the various breaks from years without repair drew the normally quiet waters of the creek swiftly downstream. From the woods emerged a little-used road that petered out in a tobacco field. A dedicated explorer could cross the field, bracing himself against the wrath of the farmer, and his car would find itself on the lane that led to the old Benner property. Winding through woods that had been cleared a generation ago to expose their natural beauty —dogwoods, azaleas and laurels had been planted among the trunks—he would not be able even to see the river for the thick growth that sucked up water from the river's edge. A natural fear of snakes would encourage him to stick to the track. Farther on would be the recreation house that old Mrs. Benner had given to her Episcopal church (she did consider that St. Stephen's was her private property) when her grandchildren refused to use it any more. They preferred the country club and its neat chlorinated pool.

Another few hundred feet downstream a numbered road crossed over the creek on an ugly wooden bridge bearing a warning that too many tons would bring it tumbling down. Beyond the bridge the creek quickly deteriorated into a maze of swampy arms, stretching among the trees and the low bamboo-like growth for half a mile until they solidified once more, became Nearing River Branch Creek again, and ran slowly, muddily across the county to join the Nearing River.

The Nearing River County sheriff stood where Father Shields had dropped his fishing rod and tried to get his bearings. A child thrown into the water in a waterproof heavy-duty plastic bag tightly tied at the top. He wondered where Jerry Sam had bought the bags. They were going to have to find out, they'd need it at his trial. He made a quick note of it.

He stooped, picked up a stick by his feet and tossed it into the water. In spite of the smooth, dull surface of the creek, the stick sped downstream. The sheriff tried following the water's edge upriver, but it was not possible. The undergrowth came right to the water, blocking foot passage. He returned to the lane. Only a very determined and well-protected body could reach the water along most of its length. He did not think Jerry Sam Hopps was either.

The lane ended slowly. It narrowed, became very rough, and then turned into two ruts separated by tall weeds. The weeds were bent over or snapped, as if a vehicle had recently driven over them. The ruts vanished at the edge of a tobacco field whose red clay was dry and exposed. It was not so dry, however, that it did not show where a car had driven right across the edge of the field to pick up the road where it disappeared into the woods beyond.

The car was parked in the sun at the edge of the pines. White station wagon, rusted out along the bottom. The sheriff and the men around him paused. It was very hot, very still. The only sounds were watery. A faint, rushing splashing sound met the sheriff's ears. For a moment he froze, thinking it was Jerry Sam and Powell. Wading? Swimming? It just was not that kind of river. Not if you had any semblance of intelligence. Drowning the other child? But at least fifteen minutes had gone by since Father Shields had climbed back into his car with the girl. Could Hopps really still be here?

"The old mill," said one of his men softly. "Water's high. Spilling through pretty fast."

Of course. He'd forgotten the old mill.

Had they taken to the woods again? Maybe the car was out of gas. Could they really be that stupid?

They fanned out, but without any real caution. The car appeared to be empty; the whole place had an empty atmosphere. There was nothing around except the heat and the insects.

"They went up the hill," called one of the men. "Left a trail like an elephant."

The sheriff dispatched most of the men to follow the trail. He checked inside the car. Empty. No traces—at least none he could spot at a glance—of Jerry Sam or Powell Hopps. The keys were hanging from the ignition.

He frowned, wondering, but wasted no time examining the car. He went back to the river. The bank was very low and damp and in a few patches free from the creeping underbrush. Very obviously Jerry Sam and Powell had stood in the mud at the foot of the tobacco field and thrown the children into the river there. There were plenty of footprints. Male sneakers. Male boot. Child's foot. And very oddly, the decorative imprint of a woman's small shoe. There'd been no report from the high school or from the Correctional Facility records of any girl friends.

A tiny shoe lay in the briars. Red sneaker with white laces. The little plastic tip on one lace was worn away and the fringe had worked out of its hole. The lace hung forlornly down in the red mud.

Next to it lay the box of plastic bags. One plastic bag,

opened but empty, had drifted over a bush and hung like laundry left to dry in the sun. The sheriff could see the fingerprints on it. He marveled at the reasoning powers that had led Jerry Sam and Powell here.

Upstream, behind a fringe of trees on the opposite bank, he caught a glimpse of the old mill. The water that roiled beneath the dam was not visibly dangerous here at the spot Jerry Sam had chosen for his disposal, but it would have grabbed the floating bag vigorously as long as the bag hadn't hung up on the very shallow water at the bank.

He looked back downstream. Father Shields had not been very far away. He and Hopps would have had no vision of each other's actions because of the density of the underbrush and a slight bend in the creek, but the plastic bag containing Lindy Davenport could have reached the priest in a very short time.

Giving artificial respiration, Martinez had said on the radio.

The sheriff tried not to hope too much. But a bag would have held a little oxygen. Kept the water out of the child's lungs. But that was assuming, of course, and it was a pitiful assumption, that Hopps had not killed the child first and then stuffed it in the bag.

It was going to be a very ugly job trying to find the remaining twin. Those currents would be treacherous. He could see, only a few yards away, a fallen tree underwater. Creek was probably nothing but wall-to-wall snags. They'd been unbelievably lucky to have had Lindy's body surface —or never sink—so fast. Randy. Well, sometimes it took divers days to locate a drowned body. Sometimes they never found it. "Yeah, Carty?" Carty was not one of his more articulate men.

"We've crossed all over that field up there, sir, real mess it is too. Looks like a woman in low-heeled shoes was there first. She wandered around in a weed field t'other side of the tobacco field and left us a path like a figure eight, and the other guys they think she was collecting weeds, you know how people do these days, weeds are kind of in. See 'em in magazines and all."

The sheriff was only half listening. He was trying to figure out the opened bag lying on the bush.

"There's a big pile of cut weeds lying at the very top of the hill. All bundled and smushed at the stem end like somebody held them there like a corsage."

"Bouquet," said the sheriff. "Corsages you pin. Bouquets you hold."

"Yes, sir. Anyway. Like women put into pots."

"Vases."

"Yes, sir. Now this pile of weeds—"

"Carty. What about Jerry Sam and Powell?"

"Yes, sir. They followed the woman, you can tell everybody was running, their prints are right on top of hers, except first she went downhill running through the tobacco field, and you can see where her heels made deep far-apart prints and then it's a little hard to tell, they all walked all over each other and back up through the weeds and all."

The sheriff sorted that out, looking down at the woman's heelprint by the creek bank. "But no signs of anybody now, I take it?"

"No, sir. There's a dirt road, but no woman, no Hoppses, no car."

He hadn't realized Carty could be so explicit. Large yellow letters on the box of plastic bags declared that it contained twelve bags. The sheriff put the box itself into a plastic bag of his own—clear, for evidence, the preserving of—and counted the remaining black plastic bags. "Ten," he said. He turned and looked into the dark river water. "Ten."

Slowly he walked back to the station wagon. Ten bags. One that Father Shields had found containing Lindy. One open on the bushes. That made twelve. That left Randy Davenport without a bag.

Using a handkerchief over his fingers, the sheriff started the engine of the white station wagon. It started immediately, with a strong motor rhythm that belied the look of the wagon itself. The needle on the gas gauge rose slowly and stopped at one-eighth.

It wasn't out of gas. It wasn't stuck in the mud.

He followed Carty through the fields on the trails made by his own men, lacing around the swath cut by Jerry Sam and company. That would be left intact as much as possible, for the experts to ponder. Jerry Sam's trail was like a neon arrow in the clay and a steam roller through the weeds.

Of course, Jerry Sam need not have bagged Randy. Just chucked him right into the water. Bagging was a bizarre sort of technique, anyway. He wondered just what the Hopps cousins had had in mind when they decided to do that.

The sheriff stared at the long straight strip of dirt road. No houses, no cars, no nothing. A pigsty, long deserted, decorated the scraggly ugly woods on the other side of the road. "We already looked," said one of the men. "Pigsty's empty. No sign that they crossed the road. Would have been a lot of mud on their shoes."

The sheriff hadn't thought Hopps would hole up in a pigsty. His men were walking down both sides of the dirt road in both directions, looking for more traces of Jerry Sam and Powell. "Probably stole a tractor," said the sheriff. "For quick and invisible transportation." There were tire marks in the grass of the shoulder where somebody had turned into the lane dividing the weed field from a huge stand of picked-over cotton.

Modern factory production, he thought. You couldn't be sure. Maybe, by some sort of machine error, the box had come with thirteen bags in it. Maybe Hopps had accidentally opened an extra. Maybe the one lying on the bushes had a hole in it or in some other way did not meet with the cousins' standards.

The heel marks left by the running woman were quite distinct. The armload of weeds, if they had had anything to do with her, had been dropped right at the crest of the hill.

Back in his own car, he put out an all-points bulletin. "Hopps and his cousin have gotten new transportation. May involve a woman picked up accidentally. No description of car or woman at this time."

Oh, lady, he thought. I hope you were here last week. Guys that drown babies. I wouldn't want to go for a whirl with them. No, sir.

Seven

I̲ₙ the Cross Hill County sheriff's office, C.D. and Laura had managed to piece together what was happening. The man Jerry Sam Hopps had broken into their home, taken their gun, and left wearing their son's clothing. He then stole a white Connecticut station wagon which contained two sleeping toddlers in the back seat. News had just come in that the toddlers had apparently both been drowned in a creek down Nearing River way.

A half-hour ago Laura had watched the attendants half carry, half usher the mother of the toddlers into a waiting ambulance that would take her to the hospital for sedation. She was suddenly reminded of slugs. Slugs had crawled across that woman's life, leaving behind slime tracks. Laura used pans of beer to drown the slugs when they tried to crawl onto her back porch. This time the slugs had not been drowned: they had done the drowning.

"I don't care if Timmy quits school," she said to C.D. She

could think of no living creature she loathed like slugs. Horrid, oozing jellylike things. Leaving a stain wherever they crawled. "It doesn't matter," she said. "He's alive, isn't he? No one drowned him in a creek."

C.D. felt no revulsion, but the rage in him was soaring, getting out of control. "They're wearing Timmy's clothes. That new shirt your Aunt Mary sent down, that's the one that Jerry Sam stole." His skin lifted with gooseflesh. Laura watched the dark hairs on his tanned forearms rise and shiver in a primitive dance.

"Shot up Zipper like he was a bale of hay and it was all target practice," said C.D. "The cops didn't want us to hear as much as we did. We only know this much because that one guy got so excited. What do you bet that Jerry Sam Hopps shot up those poor little kids, too? Then he threw them in the water."

Laura did not want to bet on that. She did not want to think about that. She wanted the words to vanish. She saw her flowerpot tipped across the broken window, saw the pellets of breakfast cereal coating the room, saw the bathroom with its drippy yellow décor. What if I hadn't had my hairdresser's appointment? What if I'd been home? Her hair prickled. She felt as if the slugs were crawling under her curls.

Poor babies, thought Laura James, poor babies.

She wept for them and for their poor mother, who was going to wake up to much worse than she'd left, and for their father, who already knew but pretended not to.

"I'm not just sitting here," said C.D., "that's for sure."

Laura could not bear the thought of going back home. She

could not possibly look at that destruction again. "I guess we could go to Harry's," she said doubtfully. She did not really want to go anywhere. In the police station it seemed not quite true. If she emerged into the hot sun and breathed in that thick damp air, she would know that it was all too real.

"I'm going out after them," said C.D.

She stared at him.

"Lot of roads out there," her husband said. "Two punks just out joy-riding. How the cops going to find them if they stay off the highways?"

"But, C.D.," protested Laura. "Those men just murdered two babies. The whole state will be crawling with cops." There was that word again. Crawling.

"Can't cover all the roads."

"They'll have to cross or use the highways sometime," said Laura.

"And in what car? Who knows what they're driving now? They dumped that white station wagon. The cops don't know what they picked up."

"Then how can you go look for them?"

"By cruising. Just like they'll be doing."

It sounded stupid to Laura. Just a waste of gas. But she wasn't going home, that was for sure, and she refused to be left by herself anywhere. Her entire body had the heebie-jeebies. Why, if C.D. dropped her at the shopping mall in Nearing River, she wouldn't even be able to enjoy that. "I'll go along," she said. "But I need something to do with my hands. And my crochet is at home."

C.D. was long used to his wife's handwork. If it wasn't crochet, it was knitting or needlepoint. "Run across the street and buy you a kit," he said. "Then we won't have to go home."

She chose a ripple afghan kit, in greens and yellows, and they got back in the pickup and drove to Harry Harlow's to get his rifle and shotgun, which they hung on the gun rack behind their heads. It did not seem at all peculiar to either of them to be loading up guns for this trip. They were a hunting family. This time it would be by road rather than field. That was all.

Laura's brother had a police-band radio that ran on batteries and C.D. had a CB radio, so they were equipped to pick up the latest news. They headed east, for the simple reason that the cops had deployed most of their forces to the south and west. Virginia had quickly closed up the northern routes.

C.D. turned on the police band, got static and began to enjoy himself.

"So tell me about your old man, Susan old girl," said Jerry Sam.

My old man, thought Susan. That would be Roger. Roger seemed part of another world. She had been in the car with Jerry Sam and Powell only two hours and already her life previous to the kidnapping seemed cloudy and surreal. The only reality was driving to the tune of Powell's skittering giggles and mumbles. "He sells computers, sir."

They did not tell Susan which road to take, only which roads not to take. Anything that looked well-traveled was out. She noted with grim amusement that she was driving west down the same road for the second time; she'd made a two- or three-mile circuit. The landscape was so featureless she wouldn't have noticed herself except that the driver always saw more than the passengers. She considered just driving endlessly around and around until somebody somewhere spotted that something was amiss.

"Yeah? You got money, then, don't you?"

Susan debated whether to claim wealth or poverty. But she had as much reasoning power as the half-alive baby wrapped in the plaid blanket. "I guess he does make a lot of money, sir," she said. "But he only gives me an allowance and I'm not really sure what he earns." Not only was that a safe answer, it was a true one. Susan's income covered the rent and utilities; Roger gave her money for food, clothing and incidentals.

"An allowance. You mean like a little kid. I wouldn't stand for that," said Jerry Sam. "You work?"

"Yes, sir." The "sir" was beginning to get to her. She was less frightened than she had been. Not that the situation was any better; it was infinitely worse to know that these two could easily murder babies. It was just that the fear seemed unable to stay at the same pitch for very long. It could, and did, return again and again with equal or greater strength, but it dissipated. The surges of fear were exhausting, like convulsions.

Right now her fear was slack. She wasn't sure if that was good or dangerous. She might lose control and get flippant and make him angry, which would be very stupid. However, if she could haul herself beyond the shaking horrors, keep that fear lying down the way it was now, she might be able to come up with some constructive thinking.

She let herself go on being annoyed with having to say "sir" to the likes of Jerry Sam Hopps.

"What do you do?"

"I'm a receptionist in a dentist's office."

"Ooooooh," wailed Powell. "I hate dentists. How can you stand that? Pawing around in other people's wet mouths all day long?"

"I don't do that. The dentist does." What would they do to her if she just stopped the car, right here in the middle of the road, with cars behind them and cars coming toward them, and told them to drop dead, she was sick of their dumb game?

But the baby. She had to remember the child. It appalled Susan that she kept forgetting its existence. And yet she must have automatically steadied the little body to keep it from being thrown from the seat during the wilder parts of the drive. It was so quiet. She slid a hand under the blanket fringe and felt the child's chest. It was warm, but then the day was warm. And the car was moving enough that she could not tell if the chest was rising and falling, or not.

Jerry Sam put his chin on her shoulder—no mean feat, with the little tan headrest in the way—and began unbuttoning the blouse she was wearing. It was a pale mint-green shirt, oxford cloth, with the sleeves very neatly rolled up and fastened with button tabs above her elbows. Perfectly matched the pin-striped pattern of the trousers and jacket she wore only in the office, where she needed it against the air conditioning. Where was her jacket? Hadn't she— Oh yes, there, on the floor. Like the baby's shirt, it had been decorated with a huge muddy shoeprint.

The top button of her shirt was undone so her necklace would show. It was a very thin real-gold chain that Roger had given her for their fifth anniversary. It was unlike him to spend so much money on her. She always thought that probably he had been fooling around at the time and felt guilty. Now she wondered about the guilty part. She did not think that anything bothered Roger enough to cause guilt.

Jerry Sam had to unbutton three buttons to get down to her bra. It was all lace—delicate, frothy and deliciously feminine. It better be, Susan had thought when she bought it, there's precious little femininity behind it to support.

She felt curiously detached from Jerry Sam's pawing hand. It was his face that sickened her, with its slimy tongue and horrid acne. Allowing for cultural differences in vocabulary, Jerry Sam said the same things about her figure that Roger said. Small, uninteresting and lacking in excitement.

Glory be, thought Susan. For the first time in my life that's an asset.

After a while Jerry Sam tired of the awkward posture he had to assume to keep up his explorations, and he sat back. Powell wanted to take a turn, but Jerry Sam said no. It was like playing cowboys and Indians. She was Jerry Sam's captive; nobody else could play with her.

Once more he and Powell discussed the escape from the roadblock. Susan listened in fascination to the newest version. They had shot at the cops. They had put bullets through the tires of pursuing vehicles. They had breathed in tear gas and survived to tell the tale.

Children, she thought in contempt, they're spoiled children who don't know how to have fun. Awkwardly, with one hand, she set to work on the buttons of her oxford shirt. The well-dressed kidnap victim, she thought, does not go about with her lingerie exposed.

"Turn right here," said Jerry Sam.

She was already past the turn. "I can't, you should have said so earlier," Susan told him. She kept on going in the same direction.

Jerry Sam slapped her. The flat of his hand caught her right cheek and ear and knocked her sideways. Her teeth punctured her tongue. The hand drew back and slapped again, more viciously.

"Hey, man," said Powell, "stop it. She's gonna go off the road. Keep your shirt on."

"Shut up, Powell," said Jerry Sam. He was halfway in the front, steering for her.

Susan was weeping with pain. She let out the clutch and gas without changing gears and the car bucked and leaped along the shoulder until the error registered and she adjusted things. The Rabbit stopped. She put a hand over her mouth. It felt as if she had severed her tongue. She could taste the awful thick salt taste of blood.

"Shut up," said Jerry Sam to her. "You call me sir, you got that, Susan?" He hit her head with his knuckles, as if he were rapping on a door and no one would let him in. She tried to block the blows with her hands, but Jerry Sam just knocked them away. "You call me sir, you hear that?" He was enraged, he was having a tantrum, she had forgotten what spoiled children did in anger, how could she have been so stupid? "Yes, sir. I'm sorry, sir. I don't know why I didn't turn, sir. I won't do it again, sir."

He stopped. He sat back and waited for her to pull herself together. Her entire skull was pounding. She panted like a dog, trying to squeeze past the pain. In the rear-view mirror, when she could focus her eyes again, she saw Jerry Sam's underfed grin crawling out between his yellow teeth.

The doctor on call was very old. He'd been sitting quietly on a high four-legged stool, resting from the ordeal of examining a three-year-old boy who'd had a little kerosene instead of his usual Kool-Aid. It turned out the little boy hadn't swallowed any, just tasted it, and he would be fine, which was luck, pure luck, said the doctor, who entertained himself for the next fifteen minutes by chewing out the mother for criminal carelessness.

When she left, sadder and poorer, he admired once more his conclusion that just because it was another generation did not mean it was a smarter generation.

He saw his pastor, burdened with a somewhat blue-complexioned child, burst into the emergency room with an energy that neither of them had exhibited in years. Mildly interested, he further observed that the policeman with Penn was from the sheriff's department, which meant the county. What had Pennington Shields been doing to get himself in trouble out in the sheriff's jurisdiction?

He was surprised to find Penn inarticulate and jumping up and down like a child needing to go to the john. Waving Penn to a chair, he allowed the cop to come into the examining room with him, assuming there would be some background here that he needed to know. The background, even to a seasoned practitioner like himself, was rather unusual.

Examining the contusions and unequal pupils, he remarked, "She's alive."

Martinez had noticed that. It had added several miles an hour to his speed.

"But not very," the doctor said cheerfully.

Martinez had noticed that too.

"Been struck pretty badly on the head. I don't handle a case as serious as this. Send her on to Duke."

Martinez didn't know why he had even bothered to come to the local hospital. It seemed to him that all the doctors there ever did was ship them on to Duke University Medical Center. He wondered where the Duke people shipped theirs to.

The ER staff took care of calling for a transfer ambulance. The doctor started IV's. Martinez retired to his car to call in. Father Shields remembered the Lord and went up in the elevator to the hospital chapel to ask His pardon and seek His help.

Yates Wolcott stared at the unholy mess on 64. The navy-blue utility van, moving over for the little beige car, had sideswiped a sedan full of old ladies going into Nearing River for a day of shopping. The old ladies had shot across the white line into the path of an oncoming semi full of furniture. The semi overturned trying to avoid them and two cars plowed into it. Which left three cars totaled, one disabled, four little old ladies on their way to the hospital, and six completely different descriptions of the little beige car's occupants.

A woman had been driving. The woman had short red

hair and sunglasses. The woman had long black hair and a scarf. There was no one in the passenger seat. There was a man in the passenger seat. The man was black. The man was white. There were two men. One of them was driving.

Everyone agreed that it was a little car and it was tan. Or beige. Or maybe white but very dirty. Except for one person who thought it was green.

Pete Williams gave a man change for a dollar for the laundromat, consisting of five dimes and three quarters. Several minutes after the customer left, smiling, Pete realized that five dimes and five nickels were rather different. Sighing, he paid back the extra from the change in his pocket. What I get for thinking about Susan Lonergan, he thought. Can't even count nickels any more.

She looked terrible. Death's door and all that. It could be the flu. Lot of people have already got it, even this early in the season. She didn't talk because she didn't want to spread any germs my way. On the other hand, you don't run around getting meals for your friends when you have the flu. Those guys were perfectly healthy-looking fellows. A little young. But still. Why didn't they go into McDonald's instead of Susan? Chivalry isn't that dead. Still has a few twitches left in it.

He couldn't imagine why she hadn't spoken to him. It had really hurt his feelings. He was embarrassed by how bad he felt over it. Maybe he should call up Susan's husband and ask if everything was all right. That was the proper thing to do when a girl you knew from high school snubbed you.

Hello, Roger, you remember me, I was two grades behind

you in school, cut classes with you once and shared detention for a week. No, they don't have detention any more, do they? Went out with narrow ties. Enough of old times, Roger old buddy. Your wife, see, is running around with two guys who aren't dry behind the ears yet and it's ruining her health, I really think you should speak to her about it.

"Yes, ma'am, we certainly do, right over there behind the potato-chip counter. A little lower. There you go."

She had exact change. How wise of her. Pete wished her a good week. Y'all come back, hear?

. He picked up the telephone and called headquarters. "Nearing River Police Department," said a cool tenor, "may I help you?"

"Yeah, man, it's me, Pete. What's happening?"

Eight

"I FEEL like an Oreo cookie," said Jerry Sam.

"Funny. You don't look like one," said Powell. They laughed.

"Didn't we just go past a country store?" said Jerry Sam. "Go back and get me a package of Oreo cookies, Susan old girl."

"Yes, sir." She stopped dead in the middle of the road without so much as checking in her mirror for traffic behind her. No crash, she thought dully, must not be anyone there. The lurch of the halting car set off her headache again. She could feel the bruises forming all over her head. Even her hair follicles were tender and throbbing. How ridiculous that sounded. She allowed herself a moment of fantasy. Poor Susan, they would say tenderly when she got to wherever they were going, she hoped it was a hospital, your hair follicles look so bruised.

It took her three tries to find reverse. Shove down. Shove left. Shove back.

It was like driving by long-distance. Her arms connected to the steering wheel, she could see how her fingers were twisted around it, but her brain was not connected to her arms. She saw the baby lying on the seat and her only emotion was envy of its unconscious state. If I could only lie down. Take a nap.

She had been decapitated along with Marie Antoinette and her head was on a pole. Some rowdy peasant was waving her head at the screaming crowds.

No.

It was just Powell, muttering "Oreo cookie" to himself.

Crazy giggles reverberated in Susan's chest, but did not escape.

"I like to split them," Jerry Sam explained to Powell. "You know, if you twist the chocolate parts just right, you don't even mess up the icing in between."

The store Jerry Sam had noticed sat alone on its barren corner, with its self-service gas pumps, brand X, and its hound dog panting in the sun. It had a sagging frame with white siding that was peeling and deadened by the sun. A few green weeds poked up along the bottom of the building. There was no solid foundation. The store rested on little piles of bricks held together by gravity. In front was a window with torn black mesh screens facing a narrow porch where a soft-drink machine and a towering pile of return bottles threatened to fall through the flooring onto the dust.

It was the kind of store Susan would never have stopped at on her own. The sort of place she would drive by, hoping her car would not choose that moment to break down. Unsanitary. Sinister in a sun-drenched rural way. Inside, it would be dark and full of flies and silent men who stared.

But once inside, she would be able to speak out loud to a real human being. She would be removed, however temporarily, from Powell's idiot mutterings and Jerry Sam's acne against her cheek.

Jerry Sam stroked her face. "Bruises don't show yet," he said, examining her with interest. "They ain't gonna look at her funny."

"How much money we got left?" said Powell.

"Forty-six of ours and thirteen of hers."

"What did we buy with two of ours?"

"The bags, stupid."

"Oh, right. I remember those." He smiled. Powell's smile, in comparison to his cousin's, was enormous. But no more pleasant. He slobbered. "Get two Cokes, too," said Powell.

"Yes, sir," she said.

Jerry Sam pulled the shotgun up and tucked it between the child's head and lap. "You want I should pull the trigger?" he asked Susan.

She had forgotten the baby again. How could she have been so callous? "No, sir," she said. So engrossed in my own pain, I forgot a baby dying right beside me, she thought. A baby. For five years I have wanted nothing so much as a baby of my own. Look at me. Temporary custody of a child and I don't even recall that it exists. Realizing the omission lessened her own physical pain and took away some of the dizziness that made functioning so difficult. It was cold water on her image of herself ("You know Susan Seton—

that dear, good, warm-hearted girl . . .") Somehow, also, it woke her to the equally cold facts of her own predicament. I will not get out of this alive, she thought, looking into the flat empty faces of her captors.

She remembered a kitten she had had as a child. Its skill was catching moths. It would bat the moths around, let them crawl an inch, and then knock them across the room. Skittling delightedly in pursuit, it would watch the moths' agonies before eating them—slowly.

All right, you two, thought Susan, do it to me if that's what you want. But not to this baby. You aren't playing that game, Jerry Sam. If I have to lie across his little body to save him when you open fire, I will do it.

She found herself sitting straighter, her teeth gripped as if Dr. Fiori were checking her overbite. How Roger would mock me, she thought. Aren't we melodramatic today, Susan? Scene stealer.

She swallowed. Can the heroics, she told herself. Start thinking instead of indulging in suicidal fantasies.

"Then don't try any funny business inside, Susan old girl." Jerry Sam moved the shotgun up and down like a lever between the baby's head and lap. He watched interestedly when the baby's head flopped.

"No, sir. I promise, sir." Susan extended her hand and made it tremble. Jerry Sam liked that, so she added a shudder. I'm learning, thought Susan, figuring out the plays.

Laura and C.D. crossed over into Nearing River County and headed east. Laura had already cast on her first row and was halfway through the second on her afghan. She did not usually look out the window when they drove. Scenery bored her. Crochet, now, all the geometric ripples slowly materializing under her fingers, that was interesting.

C.D. gathered from scraps he picked up on the police band that Jerry Sam had evaded a roadblock on a westbound highway. That meant the fellow knew north and west were out of the question.

Now east. There wasn't a whole lot to the east of Nearing River. Space. Miles and miles of nothingness stretching through ugly woods and swamps until you reached a coast so unattractive that no one lived there either. The beaches of the Carolinas, the long white miles of sand, were much farther south. South there were cities. Places to aim for. Syllables that made a punk feel good. Miami. Savannah. Wilmington.

East now. Wasn't any reason for anybody to head east. Not unless he had kin there. C.D. had learned at the police station that all of Jerry Sam's family lived up Virginia way now, except for Powell and his parents. Powell's parents hadn't cared that their son had run off with Jerry Sam. Good riddance, they said. C.D. would drink to that.

He turned his pickup truck east. Road after road after road straggling through the ugly flat countryside. He wouldn't find anyone. But at least he wouldn't be home watching Laura weep over—

Small beige car, perhaps a foreign make, said the police band helpfully.

C.D. hunched over the wheel.

Roger Seton's prime Wilmington client had lost interest. Roger tried to be courteous about it, to smile and remain good buddies and ask the guy out to lunch anyway, in spite of the fact he himself had already eaten, but he hoped the jerk would have heart failure. It made him so mad, after all this work, all these hours, all these flow charts and friendly chats—and now to have the jerk say casually they'd decided against computers, after all, kind of liked the old calculating machines, kind of got used to them, but it had been great meeting Roger, they sure appreciated his time, sure did.

He just barely kept himself from slamming the door to the man's office as he went out. It was a two-story building and the guy was on the second floor, so Roger did have the minor pleasure of stomping down each stair, letting some of the frustration pound into the steel treads.

The little receptionist downstairs beamed at him, as she always did. "Hi, honey," he said, favorably contrasting her figure to his wife's. "How about lunch?" He perched on her desk.

"I had a sandwich right here at my desk," she said, smiling. "Hours ago. But it's awfully nice of you to ask."

"Then you didn't take your lunch hour, did you, baby?"

She pursed her lips at him. Either she was preparing to put on lipstick or she thought she was cute with her cheeks all pulled in. But he was not interested in her face. "No, Mr. Seton, I didn't."

"Roger," he suggested.

"Roger," she agreed, running her tongue over her lips. That he did like. "How about an afternoon snack, then?" Roger said, choosing from his catalog of smiles one designed to tell her what he meant by an afternoon snack.

"Well," she said, considering, moving her bottom around in her swivel chair. "Maybe. If Janice would take over for me for a few minutes. It is kind of slow today."

This time they exchanged smiles.

They didn't have Oreo cookies.

Susan stared helplessly at the tobacco-chewing man in the store. He was too busy watching a soap opera on a black-and-white television that sat on a shelf across the store to notice her. She could not understand how he could be so casual delivering that news. How could he not have Oreo cookies? Jerry Sam had specified Oreos; it was the whole reason they had stopped. Fear washed over her again, leaving her weak and shaky. How much would Jerry Sam slap her this time? Or would he shoot the baby? Would that shotgun go off and leave meat where a child had been? Could a man really shoot a baby?

She supposed a man who could drown a little girl could indeed shoot a little boy. "Are you sure?" she said desperately. "I really need Oreo cookies."

Moving his jowls rhythmically around the smelly tobacco, the man hardly glanced at her. He was very fat. A white undershirt covered some of his beer belly and a pair of old khaki pants attempted to cover the rest. "I tole ya, lady. We don't have none."

She tried to lick her lips, but her mouth was too dry. A small rotating table fan faced her for a moment and hot air blew against her, drying her out even more. "May I have two Cokes then, please?" she said. It was a lengthy transaction. The fat man had to locate the Cokes blindly because he could not turn away from the screen. When she did not have exact change he told her to forget the sales tax, too much trouble, and he went on staring into the television. "Y'all come back," he said, softly so as not to drown out the dialogue.

Susan carried the two Cokes to her Rabbit, where Powell and Jerry Sam were waiting, talking, laughing, sneering. "Sir," she said, and this time the trembling required no acting, "sir, they don't have Oreo cookies." She popped the flip-tops for them. Her hand shook. Coke droplets spilled across the upholstery. Roger would not like that. "Ruin my upholstery, will you!" he'd scold. "I paid good money for this car. You maintain it properly, hear me?" But his opinion didn't matter now because she would never drive this car again. Not after Jerry Sam Hopps had rubbed his slimy flesh all over it. Not with the smell of their vile bodies ground into the corduroy of the back seat.

Jerry Sam twisted his lips. It was the most movement she had seen his face make. "Sugar wafers then," he ordered. "Whatever they've got. Just lots of cookies." He made a facial movement that could have been pleasure. My fear, Susan thought, it delights him to see my fear. That's what is putting him in a good mood all of a sudden. He's in control of me and we both know it.

"And chips," said Powell. "Potato chips, potato chips, I like potato chips. The real kind. Not pressed or garlic or taco. Just potato chips. No ridges. The kind in a bag. Potato chips."

"Shut up, Powell," said Jerry Sam.

Susan turned away from the car before they could see her shudder. It was like sucking on a lemon. No. Lemons were clean and pure and golden. There was no comparison in her vocabulary for these two, for the revulsion they aroused in her.

She crossed the dusty car lot and went back into the must and staleness of the sagging store. The fan greeted her with hot thick air and she ate a mouthful of dust it kicked up. The store was jammed with boxes and packages and display sets that once had swiveled but now were bent out of shape and sat at the front of each aisle with all the grace of dead Christmas trees. It was dark. The lights were incandescent bulbs with pull chains and few of them had been pulled. On the floor were the torn remnants of a linoleum rug. A roach ran past the counter where the country-cured hams and homemade bacon lay.

She got several boxes of marshmallow-filled chocolate-covered biscuits and a cellophane package of sugar wafers, a bag of potato chips according to specifications, two packs of bubble gum and two cylinders of Life Savers. Whatever their cravings, sugar or salt, they should be satisfied. They had not told her to get herself a drink, but she was painfully thirsty. She could feel liquid in her throat, hear the carbonation bubbling in her mouth. Very quickly she bought a canned soda and drank what she could while the fellow behind the counter bagged her purchases.

"Hot enough for you?" he said pleasantly. There was a commercial break in his soap opera. He was willing to chat with her. She had already thrown half the drink down her throat. The fizz hit the back of her nose and woke her up. "Sure is hot," she agreed.

She opened her palm to accept her change. Very slowly

the man counted it out for her. "Thank you, ma'am. Sorry about the Oreos."

"It's quite all right. Such a nice store you have here." She could not bear to stop talking, even this foolish, meaningless drivel of customer to clerk. Once the groceries were bought, she would have to walk back out the door.

I could tell him what's wrong, Susan thought. Although he seems an unlikely ally. I could barricade us in here. Shove cartons of soup in front of the door. Duck under the counter to avoid bullets coming in the window. Telephone the county police. What county were they in by now, anyway?

Except for somebody's baby lying in the front seat of her Rabbit, it was a fine strategy.

The commercial ended. Somebody in a hospital bed was forlornly returning the gaze of her intensely loving intern. "Y'all come back," said the man. "You hear?" His eyes were once again an extension of his television.

It crossed her mind that she, Susan Seton, was quite a soap opera herself this afternoon. But no one was interested. Maybe because Susan Seton was hot and wrinkled and pale and dusty. The woman in the television was cool and in beautiful repair, languishing on her pillows. Much more absorbing.

She craved just one more word from the man, but none was forthcoming. What a ritual the "Y'all come back" routine was. It had fallen out of the man's mouth without his notice. He did not care in the least if Susan came back. It was just the only way he knew to end a conversation.

"I wonder," she said politely, "if you would mind telephoning the sheriff's department for me, please."

He swung away from the soap to eye her suspiciously.

I didn't say that, she thought. The unlikely sentence vibrated in the dusty air. Now Jerry Sam will kill the baby. Stupid, stupid Susan. "Surely is hot," she said falsely, and fled. Don't come after me, take in your soap, worry about that poor lovely woman in her private room. No, please help me, please come, please, Daddy, come and take me home.

She slid quickly into the seat, handing the brown paper bag to the outstretched hands of Jerry Sam and Powell. The man mustn't come to the door to stare after her, Jerry Sam would know something was amiss. Fastening her seat belt, she left the store front so fast that gravel spurted from beneath the tires. Daddy! she thought. What made me think of him? Daddy has been dead nine years. I've popped my cork, that's what it is.

Jerry Sam and Powell were digging into the bag like children at an unexpectedly good birthday party. Not only cake and ice cream but presents too. "Bubble gum," said Jerry Sam. "I haven't blown bubbles in years. Watch this, Powell." For several minutes there was no sound but popping, giggling and chewing. When they had relearned the old grammar school technique, they each blew enormous pink bubbles, vying with each other, and then leaned forward til the bubbles touched and collapsed. "They looked like Mickey Mouse ears," said Powell. Susan thought his giggle would crucify her.

Thoughts began to click in Jerry Sam's mind. "Hey," he said. And then louder, more eagerly, "Hey!"

"What?" said Powell.

"Disney World. I've always wanted to go there. Head

south, Susan old girl. Let's drive to Florida and go to Disney World." He leaned back, chomping vigorously on his bubble gum. "We've got some cash and all her credit cards, Powell. Won't be no problem. I always wanted to go on those rides. Lots of cotton candy, I bet. When I'm at the county fair I usually buy pink."

"I'd rather go to California and see Disneyland," said Powell. He was eating potato chips at the same time he chewed his bubble gum.

"Too far," said Jerry Sam. "They got a little train affair shoots all over the place. It'll be neat."

"Yeah, but California is where the hippies are, and all the pretty girls."

"Too far."

"Aw, come on, Jerry Sam, let's go to California. I've always wanted to go to California."

Jerry Sam spat his bubble gum out the window and began tearing at the sugar wafers. The cellophane wrapping crackled noisily. "Shut up, Powell. It's too far. Blow your bubbles and shut up."

"I don't want any more bubble gum. Give me some marshmallow cookies. I don't see why you won't go to California. This car don't take no gas. And there ain't nobody'll be looking for us in California."

"Shut up!" hissed Jerry Sam. "I'm in charge. I said Florida and I said shut up."

"Aw, come on. Let's—"

"I said shut up!" screamed Jerry Sam. He hit Powell on the side of the head with the shotgun butt.

Susan clutched the wheel. There was no room in the tiny

car for a fight, especially one that included swinging a gun. She pressed herself as far forward as she could, which might have been all of three or four inches. They were on a straight stretch of road, but the Rabbit had a jittery wheel and a driver in like condition. She had to adjust it constantly; it would not cruise by itself. She hugged it, trying not to swerve, trying to obliterate the grunts and cries from her ears. Swallowing over and over again, trying not to sob, trying to remember how to play the game and not break the rules. Oh please, God, let them remember who's who. Don't let them hit me, don't let them hit the baby. What's Jerry Sam planning to do with that shotgun? Oh please, God, make him put it down.

I have to do something more intelligent than just drive. I have to do something constructive, not just barrel along here as if I'm on a Sunday fall-foliage tour. I have to stop them. It's too dangerous. For all of us.

"Susan?" said Jerry Sam peevishly.

She could not get a sound past the dry furriness of her tongue. How could so much of her be damp and the place where she needed liquid be arid as the desert?

"Susan?"

"Yes, sir."

"Susan, I think I hit Powell too hard. I think he's dead."

Nine

OCCASIONALLY she wondered about the so-called megalopolis that the news media claimed was sprawled in populous blight across the entire eastern seaboard. Of course there were towns in eastern North Carolina. But for the most part these scattered bits of civilization were sprinkled among endless woods and fields and flat scrub growth. The terrain was so low that drainage ditches sliced everywhere through the brush, in much the same way that New England is crisscrossed by stone walls. From the air, Susan thought, the farmland must resemble a massive spider web. With me for this evening's meal.

Undoubtedly the countryside was crawling with police. But somehow she had driven beyond the crawl. It was both unfair and inexplicable. I pay my taxes, she thought. And what kind of return do I get? Zilch. The cars that went by them drove faster than the fifty-five-mile-per-hour speed limit. Their occupants barely glanced at the innocuous beige car trundling along so peacefully.

Susan kept thinking of her mother. Lissie Lonergan would have handled this all so much better. No babies would have been drowned. Lissie would have managed to bag Jerry Sam and Powell back at the river, would have slung the sacks over her shoulders and toted them back to town for the police to deal with. The mere sound of Lissie Lonergan's voice would have reduced the Hoppses to trembling children.

And Susan. What had she accomplished? She had rescued nobody, stopped nothing, just sat glued to her steering wheel, letting Jerry Sam have his way. She'd wept and whimpered and trembled and driven.

Once at the dentist's office Maribeth had accused Susan of being a doormat, to let Roger behave as he did. Doormat! thought Susan. I'm the whole floor.

Even with the wind assaulting her from all windows and the sun roof, the smell was so bad Susan could hardly breathe. She had to find a place to pull over. Jerry Sam was talking to himself in the back seat.

They came to a small settlement, with the appropriate quota of shacks, stores, well-to-do houses, gas stations and a double-knit-polyester textile mill on one of its perennial shutdowns.

Here, she thought. I can stop at that gas station. There's a fuel oil tanker parked there. And a wagon full of tobacco. And their drivers standing around laughing it up with the gas station attendant. It's about time somebody dealt me a decent hand. Now I can just slide in, scoop up the baby, pop out of the car, and be home free while Jerry Sam is back there whining over Cousin Powell.

Her heart leaped. Already her muscles were planning the

order of contraction and flexion for each of these moves. She gauged the best way to sling the baby on her shoulder. I'll have to warn those men about the shotgun, she thought. Should I leap out screaming for them to get under cover, or try to put as much space between myself and Jerry Sam as possible before I yell?

She had slowed considerably, braking as little as possible, trying not to give Jerry Sam any warning of what she was doing. Her whole body felt purposeful. Her breath came shallowly. Twenty miles an hour. Fifteen. Into the gas station. No reason to bother with a full stop or turning off the motor. I don't care if the Rabbit crashes into that tobacco wagon. Just take the baby—

"Don't even think about it, Susan old girl," said Jerry Sam very softly. "Just look sorry that you drove in the wrong driveway and swing right out again and keep going."

Bastard, she thought, loathing him passionately. And I'm not much better. Chalk up one more failure for Susan Seton. You stupid ineffective idiot girl.

She gagged on another whiff from the back seat. Somebody had soiled himself. Was it Jerry Sam from panic or Powell in death? If it was Jerry Sam who'd messed his pants, he'd be enraged. Take it out on her probably. With God knew what sort of vengeance. She prayed for Jerry Sam's continence.

How did Jerry Sam know that Powell was dead? Perhaps he was just unconscious, like the baby. Jerry Sam certainly had a tendency to whack skulls. She must remember that. Must keep her skull out of his reach.

Then she remembered that he had in fact struck her too,

with his knuckles and the flat of his hand. How curious that she had forgotten. "I know how to get to a hospital from here," she said. She didn't, but there had been a small blue sign with a white arrow back at the last major intersection. She could fake it. Jerry Sam and Powell were cousins. Jerry Sam must have a high regard, even a sense of love, for Powell. If there was a chance that Powell could be saved, wouldn't he want to take it? "Or the rescue squad. They have rescue squads in a lot of these little towns. We could—"

"I'm the one tells what we could do." He was sitting up behind her again, and this time he jerked viciously on both gold hoops. Susan screamed with fear, letting go of the steering wheel to grab at her ears. The car wavered dangerously. Jerry Sam leaned over her shoulder and grabbed the wheel, steadying it. "Drive, you dumb girl. And don't make me mad again." He had a voice like sandpaper. It scraped across her nerves until they bled.

She drove.

Now she knew why she was forgetting things. Everything was repeating itself. Jerry Sam had a limited repertoire. He could hit heads, jerk earrings, shove shotguns and blow bubbles. That about summed it up. She wondered how he had ever gotten the idea to bag and drown the little children. It seemed far beyond his imagination.

"There. That tobacco shed. Pull up behind it."

It was a weathered shack, sway-backed and covered with kudzu vines. Susan loathed kudzu. Thick green vines that snaked across entire fields, engulfed trees, swarmed up telephone poles, swallowed rural mailboxes. It was like a cancer.

Its tendrils reached gleefully out to suck up whatever was in its path. Now she was going to have to drive on it. The thought was as repugnant as the thought of Jerry Sam's acne against her own cheek.

The car is stronger than the kudzu is, she told herself firmly. You've witnessed murder and beatings—you can drive over some plants without worrying that they're going to wrap themselves around the axles and trap you here in that shed with Jerry Sam.

Carefully she drove over the drainage ditch at the side of the road. It was less deep than most and the tailpipe did not scrape. The Rabbit slithered across the vines that papered the ground and stopped, puttering, behind the shed.

Tobacco sheds come in sets, as if a barn has had an undesirable litter. Three or four or five overgrown outhouses plunked down wherever they are convenient to the fields. In this group there were four. It had been years since they had seen tobacco action. The owner probably had turned to bulk curing, and in typical Southern fashion was not tearing down his useless sheds but letting them die a slow disintegrating death.

Never painted, never kept up, holes repaired with strips of tar-paper brick applied years ago when the sheds were in use, the one Jerry Sam chose had lost the last of its strength to the kudzu vine that was separating the roof from the walls. The tiny entryway was a dark hole with vines hanging over it like beads in a gypsy's parlor.

Don't make me touch the kudzu, she prayed. Her skin turned to gooseflesh.

"Get out, get out," said Jerry Sam impatiently.

She could hardly bring herself to put her foot down among the vines. The fat leaves reached up her trouser legs to stroke her bare skin. Susan shuddered violently and kicked at the awful green stuff.

As soon as she was out of the car, Jerry Sam shoved her seat forward and hauled himself out of the Rabbit by holding on to its roof. "What's the matter with you?" he said. "You trying to stomp that stuff out? Ain't nothing kills that stuff. Forget what it's called. Stand still. You're making me nervous."

She did not want to make a murderer nervous. She stood still on the kudzu and looked where Jerry Sam was looking, into the back seat of her Rabbit. Powell was slumped halfway on the floor, bent at unlikely angles, sagging in a position that seemed anatomically wrong. A swollen brown stained place marked the seat of his pants.

His head was caught up by the chin against the back of the front seat so that his eyes stared out the sun roof. The place where Jerry Sam had hit him was like a dent on an old car. Not bloody. Just misshapen.

Susan had never before seen a body prior to the ministrations of the undertakers. Powell's was probably less attractive than most, but for sheer repellency Susan ranked corpses right up there with kudzu vine.

She turned away from the car. Beyond the kudzu was an old field of corn. Brown wilted stalks that resembled an illustration of Old Testament plagues covered an area the size of several football fields before reaching the inevitable scrubby woods that framed every farm in North Carolina.

Plague, she thought. Don't wax poetic now, girl. The corn is just harvested and dying on its feet.

The sky was still beautiful. The same wisps of cloud drifted through the Carolina-blue; another jet trail was fading against it. The sun, moving down in the west, was dazzling gold.

It was only the field that was full of death and odor and crawling cancerous vines.

A car went by on the road, crammed with black teenagers. They waved at Susan, grinning at some joke of their own.

I've been kidnapped, she thought after them. I have a dying baby, a dead cousin and an escaped maniac convict with me. How's that for laughs, you dudes?

Another car went by. Two black ladies, stout, comforting-looking matrons in large iridescent hats. If they found anything peculiar about a white girl dressed for the office standing in a field and kicking vines, they didn't act on it. Whizzed right by.

Where is the famous brave knight on his white charger? thought Susan. I'm not picky. I'll take rescuers of any sex, age, race or religion.

Vaguely she recalled that she was married. That was odd. Here she was, living out every girl's nightmare, so to speak, and she had not once considered the possibility of Roger coming to the rescue, strong, virtuous, brave and true.

Well, of course, Roger was none of the above. Perhaps that was why she had not daydreamed about Roger coming dashing over the fields on his magnificent white horse. Then, too, Roger drove a Buick. People don't rescue people with Buicks. With Ferraris, maybe. With specially equipped

Rolls-Royces or purple dune buggies. But not with Buicks.

Watch it, girl, she said to herself, gritting her teeth for emphasis. You're getting punchy. Remember what happened the other times. Remember what Jerry Sam does to naughty little boys and girls. Remember the Maine. Remember the Alamo. Honk if you love Jesus.

"Help me get him out of there," said Jerry Sam.

Susan stared at him uncomprehendingly.

"Come on, come on. We can stick him in the tobacco shed. It'll be years before anyone finds him."

It would not be years. It would be minutes, when the first stray dog wandered by. "But," she said, trying to think clearly. She felt concussed herself. Normal thoughts about funerals and bereaved parents collided with shotguns and black plastic bags. "But he's your cousin. I mean, doesn't he have a mother? And, you know—people who care? They ought to have him, don't you think?"

I've driven too much without having anything to eat, she thought. It's Jerry Sam's turn to drive. I'm sick of driving.

For the first time it occurred to Susan that the oddest thing in the day's stack of odd things was that neither Powell nor Jerry Sam had expressed any desire to drive the car. They had asked about the workings of diesel engines; they had demanded that she identify all the dashboard knobs; they had been fascinated by the warm-up time required when the engine was cool. But they had not taken the wheel. Surely any red-blooded American boy would rather drive than be driven. Dubious as Jerry Sam's bloodlines were, he must crave to be behind the wheel instead of in the back seat. Or was he afraid of being seen too clearly? Of cops looking at the driver whereas they wouldn't spare a glance for the passenger?

"Yeah. My aunt." Jerry Sam sat down in the kudzu to think about Powell's mother. Susan did not see how anyone could make himself so vulnerable. That vine would crawl right up Jerry Sam's spine. On second thought, that was good. Go, kudzu, strangle him.

"But my aunt's up in Cross Hill. We can't drive up there anyway. Roadblocks. Besides, what would I say to her?"

That was a point. Hi, Aunt Bertha. Here's Powell. I saved you having to worry about him for the next fifty years. Watch it, Susan, you're getting punchy again. The only people who get away from their kidnappers are cool, calm and collected. Which lets me out. I've popped my cork.

"I still think Florida would be a nice place to go." Jerry Sam picked at the vine, daydreaming about Florida. For a few seconds his plastic face seemed less vicious.

I could run away from him. The town isn't but half a mile back.

Experimentally Susan lifted a foot. It was very heavy. She doubted if she could totter to the edge of the road, let alone outdistance Jerry Sam for half a mile. Not to mention the shotgun. And the baby still folded up like a rag doll on the front seat.

The baby was somebody's child. No one was worried about Susan Seton, nobody even knew she was missing. No one was waiting for her to show up at work or have a meal ready for dinner. But somebody, somewhere, must be crazy with fear for the little boy. And the other one, his sister, in the black plastic— No, I'm not going to think about that I'm not, better to be punchy, Roger darling, faithless Roger, where is your shining steed now when I need it?

"If we can kind of drive sideways for a few hours," said Jerry Sam, ripping kudzu leaves in shreds (what powerful fingers he has, thought Susan, but I knew that already, my ears, my poor ears), "we can sneak out of the area and get back on the highway and head for Wilmington. That's on the way to Florida."

Driving sideways didn't sound any harder than driving in circles. Susan's hysteria began to bubble to the surface. Giggles rising like yeast came out of her chest. She tried to swallow them, the way she swallowed when she was close to throwing up, but the giggles were more tenacious. They percolated through her closed teeth and snorted out. Jerry Sam glared at her. "Shut up. You sound like Powell."

Her laughter, like Powell's, splattered to a stop, choking on itself.

Jerry Sam took his cousin by the shoulders and jerked until the body flopped partway out of the car. It didn't seem to bother Jerry Sam at all that the head kept getting caught on the hinges of the driver's seat. He just pulled until the head ripped on past.

Susan covered her ears. She could feel them ripping in sympathy. Sympathy with Cousin Powell. That was rich.

"Take his feet, Susan old girl."

She bent over Powell's body. The feet were extraordinarily far away. I'm going to faint, she thought. It meant falling into the kudzu or onto Powell. She really did not know which would be worse. Don't faint, don't, don't.

"You pass out on me and I'll wake you up with a pair of

scissors," said Jerry Sam. His voice was tight again, strangling her, jerking on her like a rope.

She took Powell's ankles and together they dragged the body over to the shed. Tobacco drying sheds had small framed openings low on one side but not usually any real doors. It would be a job to get Powell's body through the hole. Susan tripped over some tobacco sticks among the rubble and lost her grip. Silently Jerry Sam waited for her to hoist the ankles again. She bumped into the old fuel tank rusting on its metal legs outside the shed and steered herself to the little flap door. Jerry Sam had an uncomplicated way of dealing with difficulties. Susan watched him in warped admiration as he kicked at the opening until the entire side of the shed sagged to let him pass. They staggered in, dropped Powell onto the dirt floor, right next to the stove, and backed away before the shed fell in on top of them.

Rats, thought Susan. There are rats in there. I was wrong. A passing dog won't find him first.

She stumbled back to the car and clung to the door handle for support, vomiting all over the waiting kudzu.

"Hurry up," said Jerry Sam. "We got to hit the road. Cops must be all over the place by now." He shoved her into the driver's seat and slammed the door on her. Then he went around to the passenger side. He paused for a moment, looking at the baby, which had not objected to being squashed each time the seat was folded forward.

"Don't hurt him," pleaded Susan. "Don't hurt him, please. He's someone's baby. Someone loves him." I wish I had a baby. I wish Roger—

"Okay. I need him anyhow. Keeps you in line." Jerry

Sam picked up the child and dumped it on the back seat.

Like groceries, thought Susan. Like meat. He has no more regard for the baby than for the cats by the railroad tracks.

Jerry Sam plopped into the front seat. Now there was nothing between them except the stick shift. And it was a very small, short stick. He grinned at her, as much as his lips would allow, and then he stroked her knee. But there was nothing left in Susan's stomach to vomit.

She turned on the motor, taking advantage of Jerry Sam's preoccupation with her knee to click off the radio. The hard angry singing and twanging guitars of the radio stations he liked scraped her nerves raw. Jerry Sam did not appear to notice the lack of sound. She clenched her fingers around the wheel, getting rid of some of her tension, and put the diesel into reverse.

Bumping over the ditch to the edge of the road, Susan waited until a couple of cars and a pickup truck whizzed by. Then she backed into the traffic lane, moved into first and accelerated. Out of the corner of her eye she saw the kudzu vines on the tobacco shed trembling in the breeze. Rats, she thought. No, I won't think about rats in there with Powell. Just like I'm not thinking about black plastic bags and rape and shotguns. Drive, drive, drive.

Ten

THEY had caught it from the chief, from the SBI and now, praise the Lord, the FBI was taking its turn. Yates Wolcott stood there with Merton and Bloom and tried to think about his wife's garden, which was full of autumn gold chrysanthemums and purple aster.

They weren't interested in his excuses. If he was really lucky, they'd tell themselves, "Dumb country cops, what did we expect?" and go take care of Jerry Sam Hopps themselves. It was fine with Yates. He had no proprietary feelings toward the Jerry Sams of his world.

It just seemed to Yates that while they were picking on people, they might say a few words against the guards at the Correctional Facility. Those guys weren't exactly lily-white these days either.

Yates mentioned casually that he had had two grocery-store robberies since noon, and what with them and the pileup on 64, he'd had his hands full and he hadn't delegated responsibility because there was no one to delegate to.

The SBI and the FBI leaped all over his grocery stores. It was Merton who explained carefully that because the robbers had been black, he and Bloom and Yates tended to think they hadn't been Jerry Sam and Cousin Powell, especially since Jerry Sam specialized in gas stations. The FBI muttered skeptically to itself until Bloom concurred. Bloom was black, and that lent authenticity to Merton's claim.

Yates thought longingly of being a cop in New York City. In New York, when their shifts ended they went home. Trust New York to think of an innovation like that. Those Yankees were smart. Yates understood that they actually complained about it, though. That was not smart. If they transferred him, Yates, to New York, they wouldn't catch *him* complaining when it was time to go home. At this rate the chrysanthemums would be wilted and gone before he ever had a chance to stand before them in admiration.

The man's name was Bros. Short for Brothers, because he ran a store called Peterling Bros. There was not and never had been a brother.

Bros drove a Cadillac himself. It saddened him that cars were getting shorter and more squat every year. He'd kept his Caddy four years now, much longer than he liked, because the new ones just didn't have that sleek look any more. Bros never wanted to end up with some ugly little tuna-fish can on wheels, like that thing the redhead was driving. All her windows open, too. Bros had never opened the windows on his Cadillac, except for the drive-in teller at his bank, and that didn't count. You drove around with your windows open, everybody knew you were too poor or too stupid to get a car with central air.

The girl didn't look poor, she'd been pretty in a dishwater sort of way, but she was evidently one of the stupid ones. You met a lot of weirdos in a grocery store—they all had to eat—but Bros couldn't remember anybody getting tears in their eyes because he didn't carry Oreo cookies.

I wonder if you would mind telephoning the sheriff for me?

Bros spat, shifting the tobacco wad from his left cheek to under his lower lip. He played with it with his tongue, and a yellowy dribble appeared at the corner of his mouth.

The girl had taken off fast enough. Bros didn't think much of two guys letting a girl drive them. Get their food, too. Take two trips hiking back and forth with their drinks and their snacks.

He thought it was probably a gag. Though she was getting old for teenage tricks. What the hell, thought Bros. Slow day.

He picked up the phone and dialed the Cape County sheriff.

"Hey! That car back there," said C.D. excitedly, turning down the volume on his CB radio. "The one backing out of that field, did you see it, Laura?"

Laura nodded. Occasionally she glanced up from her crochet. She was doing a green row. The kit colors were brown, rust, forest-green, mint-green and lemon-yellow. It was quite cheerful. She certainly didn't feel good about any of this, but she felt better. If her fingers were busy, her nerves were under control. She must have made thirty afghans in the last decade. The couch back of every single person to whom she was related was decorated with one of her afghans. Afrigans, she pronounced it. She had a vague feeling the slaves had brought the skill with them from Africa.

"Beige. Little. Foreign," said C.D., tickled by the sound of his list. "That's what they're looking for, all right. I'm going back and check them out."

"There was a girl driving it," said Laura. "Leave the poor thing alone, C.D. You're going to give some woman heart failure, stopping her car and running around waving your shotgun in her face."

"It's her passenger I'm interested in. Young. Looked like a punk."

"You can't tell that someone's a punk just by driving by."

"Yes, you can. Remember that friend of Timmy's, when he was in seventh grade? You just took one look at that complexion, those runty eyes, that greasy hair, and you knew he was a punk."

Laura was thinking that they could just sell the brick house. She'd visited a friend in a new double-wide trailer and it was cute as the dickens. They hadn't decorated in Williamsburg either; they'd chosen French providential, and it was mighty handsome. White and gold and curlicued. It wasn't as if she and C.D. were land-hungry. They could put up a mobile home anywhere. Have a well dug. Septic system. It would be new and smell clean and not be trespassed upon, and she would always, always lock the doors. She'd have another dog, and that dog would be on a chain by the front door and nobody, but nobody, would go in

Laura James's house unless Laura James told the dog to hush.

C.D. stopped the pickup and made an awkward U, for a moment blocking the opposite lane. He paused there until the little beige car came tootling up in the other lane. C.D. grinned to himself. Then he reversed the pickup truck sharply to block both lanes.

Pete Williams hit every single red light in Nearing River on his way to the police station. He could hardly take a solid breath between his rage at himself for letting Susan walk by him into the arms of those animals and his rage at the lights for turning red when he, Peter Williams, wanted to surge through the traffic.

They'd been sitting right in the back seat of her car, not ten parking spaces from the door where he'd stood and watched her. Wasting time with his stupid hurt feelings and not seeing things as they were at all.

"I have her name and her license number," he said. They put it over the police wave. Volkswagen Rabbit diesel, two-door, beige, the driver positively identified as Susan Seton, age about thirty-three, five feet three inches, less than a hundred pounds, red hair, brown eyes, green pants and shirt.

At least he'd noticed her clothes.

He was feeling better. A four-hour nap, a light lunch of chunky soup and crackers, and Dr. Fiori felt he could face the world again. Must not have been death's door, after all. Just a minor cough. Brought on by stress and overwork.

He'd call Susan and tell her tomorrow was a workday.

But Susan's phone did not answer.

He called Gayle and Maribeth, his chairside assistants. "So we'll be working tomorrow, regular hours," he said. "Try to get in touch with Susan, will you?"

Gayle and Maribeth promised to try to get in touch with Susan. Dr. Fiori put down the receiver and planned the rest of the day. It was a toss between a few beers out on the redwood deck in the afternoon sun or a cup of hot soothing tea here in the kitchen. Then maybe he could start in on that new mystery the book club had sent, or go down to the courts for a little tennis practice.

The phone rang.

"Dr. Fiori," he admitted. His breath didn't catch and no cough started up. Good. It was under control.

"Dr. Fiori, this is Officer Peter Williams of the Nearing River Police Department? I need some information from you about your secretary, Susan Seton."

"Susan?" He was completely amazed. If ever there was a law-abiding body, it was surely little Susan. "Is something wrong?"

"We're not sure, sir. We'd like to get in touch with her husband. Can you tell us how to reach him?"

Dr. Fiori could not. He had never even met Roger Seton. Knew nothing about the man. Salesman, or some such thing. Gayle or Maribeth might know more.

"Yes, sir. Can you give us names of relatives in town or out of town whom we could call?" Pete had looked in the phone book. There were no Lonergans listed and only the one Seton.

"Her father is dead, her mother's in Greensboro," said Dr. Fiori, "and her brother is in Richmond. I think she has some family still living around here, but I don't know their names. Her maiden name was Lonergan, if that helps."

It didn't. Dr. Fiori had no first names, no phones and no addresses. But perhaps the chairside assistants could give Pete some information. Whatever a chairside assistant was.

Roger Seton paid for a strawberry-and-cream pie and two cups of coffee for the receptionist and a cup of coffee for himself, and the little twirp up and thanked him for it and sashayed right back to the office. No, she couldn't see him tonight, she was busy. Roger nearly hit her. He was so annoyed he didn't leave a tip for the waitress, who was fiftyish and overweight anyhow.

On the fourth phone call Pete Williams found out Roger's company and the company helpfully said that Roger had a pretty free hand; they didn't expect to hear from him more than twice a week, and no, they really had no idea where he might be right now. Well. If it was truly as important as all that, they supposed the officer could try Goldsboro, Jacksonville or Wilmington. Mr. Seton had some contacts down that way he was trying to line up. Yes, they were fairly big towns. No, they couldn't narrow it down much more than that.

Normally these calls were so routine as to be unmarked in Pete's memory. It was just a job. But this time he was at fault. He had let Susan get back in her car when he knew perfectly well that something was radically wrong. Flu. Nobody had flu in October. Pete pressed the supervisor, pressed the supervisor's supervisor, and finally got out of them the name of the motel chain that Roger preferred. "Mind you, he might not be in any of those cities," said the telephone. "He could be in South Carolina. Hell, he could be home taking a nap, for all I know."

"Thank you, sir," said Pete. They had already tried the apartment. He began calling motels in Goldsboro, Jacksonville and Wilmington. He got Roger's motel on the eleventh call and they rang Roger's room for him and on the ninth ring Roger picked it up.

Pete identified himself.

Roger's voice rang with camaraderie and old times. "Pete! You old son of a gun. What's happening? How are you, anyway?"

It was quite unusual for a policeman to call somebody long-distance and get a relaxed sociable response like that. Most people panicked, fearful that someone was hurt or that they'd unknowingly done something wrong and been caught. First thing you had to do was reassure them that they had done nothing wrong and you just wanted a little information. He was amazed that Roger's first remark had not been to see if his wife was all right.

"There's been some trouble here," said Williams. "A guy doing time for robbing gas stations escaped from prison, and we think that the car he and a cousin of his got hold of is your wife's diesel Rabbit."

"Aaaaah, Jeez," said Roger. "They can go a million miles in that. It gets fantastic mileage. Damn. What did that stupid

Susan do? Leave the keys in the car? If they ruin my upholstery—"

"Roger, we think your wife was in it when they took it.
We think they're making her do the driving for their escape."

Roger was silent for a moment. Then he said doubtfully,
"Susan's not much of a driver."

Pete cast his eyes to heaven, in the form of a much-
cracked plaster ceiling that needed spackle and paint. "She's
a hell of a good driver, from all the reports we're getting,"
he said. "The point is, she is in real and terrible danger.
These two men have committed at least one murder since
escaping from the Facility."

At last Roger began expressing concern at his wife's predicament. He and Pete exchanged worried phrases, and Pete
got down to the business of getting information about any
friends or family Susan might be forced to drive to.

"No," said Roger. "She just doesn't have any family lo-
cally. Even distant cousins. I have lots of kin, but they're
over Asheboro way. Wrong direction."

"If they head south or east, where would she be most apt
to go as a place she would see as safe? Does she know any
towns besides Nearing River especially well?"

"What would she have to do with the decision?" said
Roger. "They must be telling her where to go."

"We don't think they know where to go."

Roger considered this. "Susan wouldn't know where to
go either," he said. "I always do the driving when we take
trips. She has a bad sense of direction. She's always going
in circles. She never remembers highway numbers. She's

always setting off on 97 when she wants 64. If she decides where they'll drive, they won't get very far." He laughed.

"And her brother?" said Pete, not caring for the laugh. "How can we get hold of him?"

"Why do you want David?"

"Just trying to notify people, Roger."

"Oh." He supplied a business phone for David Lonergan in Richmond, Virginia.

"How about her mother, Mrs. Lonergan?"

"I don't know her number," said Roger. "Take my advice and don't even call her. The old bag'll run your whole shooting match if you do. She's in Greensboro, I know she's listed, because she'd never risk missing a telephone call."

Another nice close family. Pete scribbled in his notebook. Another thought struck him. "Do you have any children?" he said. "We'll need to send somebody to get them at school."

"No," said Roger, "I'm not very fond of kids."

Pete was not surprised. "Where can we reach you with any news?" he said. "Will you be driving up to Nearing River?"

"Gee, I don't know," said Roger Seton. "I mean, what could I do?"

The owner of the mobile home brought his usual brown paper grocery bag out to clean the debris off the shoulder of the road. Every day there were beer cans and soft-drink cans and fast-food-joint discards. Waxed papers, paper cups, halves of hamburgers.

Today it was a pile of wet smelly children's clothing.

"I knew mothers threw out the diapers these days. See 'em advertised on television," he said to the tiger lilies, which someone had decorated with a used Kleenex. "But I still thought you hung on to clothes at least till the kid outgrew 'em."

He shrugged. Plastic. A whole generation of disposables. He stuffed the nasty clothes into his bag, carried the bag to his garbage can behind its little screen back of his trailer, and compacted the day's accumulation with his foot. Then he hurried inside to scrub the contamination off his hands.

Susan slammed on the brakes, the full weight of her body lunging against the seat belt. It wrapped against her strongly, competently, leaving her free to keep the wheel straight. Her head started throbbing again. Her knee shook from the force she was applying to the brake pedal.

Jerry Sam was not so lucky. He had refused to attach his seat belt, contending, with truth, that it prevented complete freedom of movement and a man had to be free. He was thrown against the dashboard, desperately ducking and padding his collision with his outthrust hands. Susan heard a distinct clunk where his head struck the dash, and when she could manage it, she turned to examine the injury. But the only visible damage was to Jerry Sam's pride.

She had stopped the Rabbit no more than ten feet from the pickup stalled across her lane. After all of today's trials, it seemed ridiculous that once more her body responded with jelly joints and shuddering stomach. You'd think by now I'd be used to catastrophe, she said in silent disgust, but no. Still the shaking Victorian maid.

A man vaulted out of the pickup and ran the few steps over to the Rabbit. He was a big barrel-chested fellow with a bloated beery look and small black eyes. He had a shotgun.

What had happened to her world? Was there no one left in it but gun-toting Jerry Sams? Who was *this* one?

I'm the jam in the sandwich, she thought. He and Jerry Sam are going to spray each other with buckshot and I'm going to be the one that gets riddled with holes. Yesterday the only people I knew read magazines in a dentist's waiting room. Today they all have shotgun fetishes.

The seat belt kept her from sinking to the floor. She found the release with her right hand and sprang herself free from it so she could ball herself up and make herself small.

Just before she screwed her eyes shut she saw a woman leaning out of the pickup holding a crochet hook, a woman with frosted blond hair teased in a dated beehive. It was definitely a crochet hook, Susan saw it clearly. It just doesn't go with shotguns, she thought, one of us is on the wrong track. The woman took in the two shotguns facing each other. "Seedy," screamed the woman. Susan sank out of sight. "Seedy! The man's got a gun, you know he'll use it, Seedy, look out!"

Jerry Sam popped out of the sun roof like a cartoon character emerging from a manhole, leveled his shotgun at the man and blew him to shreds with a blast that shattered the remnants of Susan's hold on sanity.

The silence that followed was surreal. Susan listened to the distinctive puttering of the diesel engine. It was like a train going over the tracks; it was saying Shoot 'em dead, shoot 'em dead, shoot 'em dead, shoot 'em dead.

Jerry Sam fell down through the hole.

I got it backward, thought Susan, stunned. The man shot Jerry Sam, it's Jerry Sam filled with bits of metal. If I can just huddle down here a little while longer, everything will be all right. Seedy. What a dreadful name. But so suitable. He looked seedy.

"Drive, dammit, drive," said Jerry Sam. "Can't you see there are cars stacked up in each direction? We got half of North Carolina watching this!" He jerked on her shoulders, pulling her out, turning her around, placing her fingers on the steering wheel.

The man's body was lying across the hood. It was hideous, like a scene from a bad color movie about the FBI's most wanted. "I can't drive," she said, gesturing at the man, "he's on my hood."

"He'll fall off," said Jerry Sam impatiently. "Just step on the goddamn accelerator."

"But I might run over him."

"So what? He's dead, he ain't gonna feel it."

She was crying again. What reservoir was producing these tears? She had had nothing to drink for hours. She was dehydrating herself by crying and vomiting. She'd be the next one to die. She'd just tip over here at the wheel and the car would go off the nearest cliff. But there were no cliffs in North Carolina. Just flat fields with drainage ditches.

I can't die, she remembered with clarity. There's the baby. I still have my baby back there. And its mother. Its mother is expecting me to do something intelligent.

She wiped her nose on her sleeve again. This time she barely noticed. She put the car in first gear and edged past the pickup. The woman had vanished. Susan hoped she was on the floor, alive and unhurt. With her crochet hook.

The body lay across the hood. It had fallen so that the bulk of its weight was on the car. The legs dangled over the road. At least the face was away from her. She had to see the hair and the perforated torso, but the face was underneath, pressed up against the metal of her car.

She knew what Roger would say. She could just hear him, in that cross voice of his: "Get that corpse off of there. It'll ruin the finish."

"For the love of Pete," said Jerry Sam. He wasn't angry, wasn't cursing. He was exasperated. Dead bodies do the silliest things. He stood up through the sun roof again and shoved the body off onto the cement with the butt of the shotgun.

Susan closed her eyes and drove blind for several yards. When she opened them she saw three cars lined up waiting behind the pickup, watching Jerry Sam's body-disposal technique. Jerry Sam grinned at them, waving his shotgun. Nobody seemed to want to interfere. She moved into second gear, third, fourth, and shot ahead to the next intersection to head south.

Eleven

THEY stopped at the first gas station they came to so Susan could go to the bathroom and Jerry Sam could stock up on soft drinks from the machine.

When she got back into the car he told her to forget the speed limits. Whatever this Rabbit would do, do it. Eighty, ninety, whatever. Get a move along.

She drank from her flip-top ginger ale. The bubbles attacked the back of her nose, but at least it was liquid. Wonderful, wonderful liquid. And the baby? What about him? He has to have something too. I have to do something about the baby.

She got up to eighty-five, but it was too scary. The cars going fifty-five materialized so fast she couldn't gauge her distance. She dropped back to seventy-five.

"Jerry Sam, listen. I'm going to make you a promise. I promise to do whatever you want, and I mean whatever, really, completely, if you let me put the baby with someone who'll take care of it. I don't care where. We can just stop at the next gas station and I'll set it on the pavement. We don't have to go to the hospital or the rescue squad or anything like that. Just let me give the baby to anyone, anyone at all."

"No. And listen to me. I've let you get away with lousy language. You're calling me sir, remember? Remember that, Susan old girl?" He took the shotgun and rammed the barrel between her legs. The brief bravado vanished. "Yes, sir," she said, quivering.

He grinned. She hated the grin. She wanted to take the lips and stretch them, like a real person's, make his plastic skin move.

"Sir?"

"Yes?" he drawled.

They had come to a crossroads. She did not think she had the strength to shift gears one more time. She could barely turn her head to check for traffic. The motor idled at the stop sign. So did her brain.

"I . . . I'm tired, sir. I can hardly drive." It took no effort to make her voice shake. She checked the mileage. They had not been driving forever. All this cruising, all this running, all her circles and confused turning—and they had gone barely ninety-five miles. She could not believe it. Surely they had gone hundreds and hundreds of miles. "Won't you drive?" she said. "Please, sir?"

He would tell her that if he drove she would be able to get away. She would tell him that on the contrary, she couldn't get out of a moving car, he'd be going eighty,

eighty-five anyway, she'd be as stuck as if he were holding the shotgun on her.

Jerry Sam was silent. She turned to look at him and he averted his face from her gaze. She might have been catching him in some immodest act. He played with his belt buckle and fidgeted with the maps piled on the shelf of the dashboard. Finally he said uneasily, "Never drove a stick shift."

"You haven't, sir?" said Susan almost gaily. "Well! Why don't I teach you? We've put a dozen miles between us and . . . and what happened. Let's go down some side road and find an old dirt lane and practice. It won't take long to learn, sir. You'll like driving this Rabbit."

Her enthusiasm rang like a cracked bell. The same tone of voice she used with young dental patients, telling them it won't hurt, you'll be just fine. When she and they knew perfectly well it would hurt terribly and they would not be fine.

"Well," said Jerry Sam.

She beamed at him. "Now this," she said, moving the stick in her right hand, "this is neutral. Feel it? Feel how it sort of jiggles around in there with lots of room?"

Jerry Sam felt neutral.

"There!" said Susan brightly. "That's the most important one, sir. And you've already got it. How about that?" She could hear her voice moving falsely around in an unfamiliar key; it must be rasping on Jerry Sam like Powell's giggle. But Jerry Sam grinned between his slit lips and said, "Okay. Good. You can teach me."

The time they could waste! Sitting in one place. It was like being lost in the woods. They always said stay in one place and we can find you, just don't move around. Here, cops, cops, cops, cops. Come and get it! Susan's got Jerry Sam cornered for you.

She beamed at him again.

He reached over and jerked violently on her earrings.

The tears were back, and the pain, and the fear. "Why did you do that?" She was screaming at him. She could not control her voice.

"Because you were getting cocky there, Susan old girl. I may not be able to drive your heap, but, honey, I'm in the catbird seat here and don't you forget it."

David Lonergan's office furniture seemed to sway and turn into drunken zoo-shaped creatures. He gripped the white phone in his left hand and supported his head with his right. "What?" he said dizzily. "What did you say?"

He could not remember a Pete Williams. But they had established that David had graduated from Nearing River Senior High with Pete's older cousin Willis Williams. David remembered Willis clearly. Basketball. The Williamses lived over beyond the park near the bend in the river at the highway. So Pete had become a cop. How about that. And then, having established his bona-fides, the cop got to the point of the call.

David could not absorb the description Pete Williams gave him of Susan's day. Domestic, puttering, busy little Susan, his baby sister. Carting two hoodlums across eastern North Carolina while they drowned toddlers and held up gas stations. "I'm on my way," said David. "Don't let them hurt her till I get there."

148 · Caroline B. Cooney

"No, sir," agreed Pete.

"I didn't mean that. It didn't come out right. I meant, I'm coming and you make sure she doesn't get hurt. Until I get there." That didn't sound right either. "I mean—"

"I understand, Mr. Lonergan. We're doing everything we can. How do you plan to get here?"

David pulled himself together. It would help Susan not at all if he disintegrated. Richmond was a two-hour-and-forty-minute drive, and right now—he clicked the tiny knob on the side of his digital watch—it was four forty-seven. He wouldn't get there until after seven-thirty. The sun would be going down. You couldn't do anything after the sun went down. If those guys had Susan after dark—

"I'm flying down," he said.

The officer was doubtful. "There aren't many flights, sir," he said. "I don't know if you can get a connection quicker than you could drive. If you decide to drive, just keep calm and observe the speed limit and the red lights. It won't help Susan one bit to have you wiped out in an accident."

Patronizing small-town cop, thought David furiously. Telling me how to drive. Quickly he blanked out the vision of himself tearing at high speeds through the small towns littering the highways between Richmond and Nearing River, scattering all and sundry, with one hand pressed on the horn and the other skillfully guiding the wheel of his racing chariot. "I'm flying," he repeated. "If I have to, I'll charter a plane."

The officer was suitably impressed by that. David was suitably impressed by that. He had never in his life considered chartering a plane. It was a phrase out of television. He said good-bye to Pete Williams and dialed the Air Taxi.

. . .

Henry Davenport's world did not stop swaying just because he told it to. His daughter was badly injured and on her way in an ambulance to a university medical center for specialists to treat her. Lindy. Silly, giggly, thumb-sucking Lindy. Who was supposed to grow up into the loveliest, smartest, best big girl a daddy ever had. Lindy. Please, God, let her not be that badly hurt.

He began to cry, and they lowered him into a chair and just stood there and let him go on crying. Henry could see Disney World and Lindy and Randy screaming with delight when he held them in his arms on one of the rides. He could see the camera filled with color film as he aimed it at his babies, dressed in their matching outfits, standing next to Mickey Mouse and Donald Duck. But mostly he could see Janelle, still asleep in the hospital bed, not yet knowing.

"And Randy?" said Henry. "They're twins, you know. Where is Randy?"

They didn't know.

"If you found Lindy, you found Randy," said Henry, to whom the children were an indivisible set.

They were sorry, sir, they hadn't.

"But what's going on?" he said frantically.

We're doing our best, sir. Just stay here with your wife.

Henry, halfway out of the room, said, "But I have to go to this Duke place with Lindy."

They wouldn't let him. They told him they were working on it. He was left there, knowing nothing, doing nothing. They'd work on it. And what was he supposed to do? Play bridge?

They brought a different doctor for Henry. Much younger, very strong. But the tranquilizer had the same effect.

Felicity Lonergan checked herself in the mirror at the top of the stairs and was pleased. Her chest had expanded over the years until it was of Wagnerian proportions. For several decades she had fought the change, but now she was satisfied with herself. The shelf that her bosom had become was useful in many regards. Right now it was a fine place on which a scarf and its stickpin and three long chains of delicate filigreed gold could repose. At other times she employed it as a scraper. When people got in her way, she simply directed her prow toward them and scraped them out of the room. It was very effective. In her twenties she had used her figure to bring men closer; now she had only to surge forward and they fell back. Felicity did not mind at all. She was a New Woman. Men interested her not in the least.

She had mourned properly for Frank, of course, and even missed him in a desultory way. But the marriage had become an old vehicle that was comfortable and familiar but which neither of them minded trading in. Well, no, it was hardly fair to speak for Frank. He might have minded very much trading in. After all, it was Felicity who got the new life, while poor Frank's came to a halt.

She had moved away from the little neighborhood where she and Frank had lived for several years, and found herself an apartment near the campus and was going back to college. It was wonderful fun. The students were crazy about her. She was a moving, breathing lovelorn-advice column. It was the most satisfying part of a life that had been on the whole very good anyway.

Frank and their old friends had always called her Lissy. Lissy Lonergan had made cookies for Brownies and chaired committees at church and been a patron for the spring fashion show and given Christmas coffees famous for the variety and taste of their handsome spreads.

Now she was Felicity. No one had ever called her Felicity. It suited her stout, strong profile. It sounded competent and capable. She much preferred being Felicity.

It was Felicity who had wandered about the entire campus, exploring every laboratory and classroom and nook and cranny, and come upon the pottery section at the New School. That was a foolish cognomen. The New School was the division of the university that taught such pleasant things as basket weaving (yes, truly, they had a course in it; you could even take it for credit) yoga, nutritional analysis of junk foods and pot-throwing.

She loved the idea of throwing pots. She saw herself standing in a target room and hurling a piece of crockery at the silhouette of a wanted criminal. The class didn't turn out to be precisely like that, but in its own wet, messy, clay-y way, pot-throwing was extraordinarily satisfying. Felicity prided herself on throwing some very fine pots.

The problem was what to do with them. She took along a few cartons full every time she went to visit Susan, and Susan, always courteous, always the sweet daughter, would ooh and aah and thank her so much. Felicity was positive there was not enough room in that small apartment for all the pottery she'd given Susan. Susan was probably the largest supporter of the Christmas bazaars in Nearing River. Probably if she sauntered in to the Episcopal Churchwomen's Annual Christmas Craft Gathering, she'd find an entire table of her own pottery, at five dollars a mug.

Felicity did not mind. One cause was as good as another. Just as long as she didn't have to organize them any more, that was all she asked.

She was on her way to her class in twentieth-century music. She did not know when she had enjoyed anything so much. Last week they got to pluck piano strings and whack gongs with glasses which broke with a pretty tinkle that your companion in the arts picked up on his microphone, the one he was scratching with a hairbrush. They had listened to some recordings of John Cage, which their instructor had classified under "Theatre of Aimless Activity," and one of the recordings had been blank. People were actually paying cash money to buy a blank record.

Felicity loved it. What a con. What a man. Actually masquerading his garbage as art and making a profit yet. Now that was pizzazz. She hoped today's class would be as good.

The telephone rang as she was going out the door.

Never once in her entire life had Felicity been able to let a phone ring without answering it. She bounded back into the apartment—answering phones was the only time in which she bore any resemblance to her son-in-law Roger; her pink box of flesh would cross the room like a Marine going to chow—and picked it up happily. Any time anyone wanted to talk to Felicity Lonergan was a good time.

"Hello?" she said. "For heaven's sakes. Little Peter Williams. Of course I remember you. I had to spank you once at a Cub Scout Free-for-All. No, they didn't call them that, did they? What were those Cub Scout things? How are you, Peter dear? So you grew up, after all. You were one of the ones I had my doubts about. Are you in town? Come have supper with me. It's all made. A vat of potato salad with lots of crisp bacon thrown in. I'll get steaks out of the freezer. We'll have a reunion . . .

"Oh. You're not in town. What a shame. Why, Peter, I was going to cut my classes just for you. Did you know that I'm going back to school? It's such fun. You must quit work and go back to school."

She could not recall who it was Peter had married and therefore had financial obligations to. "Jane Simon?" she repeated. "Peter, I don't believe I knew any Simons." She was affronted. Nearing River was full of new people these days; she'd been away for thirteen years and they'd spent that time filling the woods with subdivisions and strangers. And here was little Cub Scout Peter Williams married to some girl she didn't even know. "Well, I swan," she said, dropping back into her Nearing River dialect. "Do you have any children of your own, Peter?"

Peter seemed to be having a hard time functioning at his end of the line, but she was able to grasp that he was now a policeman. "I think that's just fine, Peter," she said. "I'm a great supporter of law and order. I saw a bumper sticker about that just the other day and I very nearly ordered one for myself. It was obscene, though, and I haven't quite reached the stage of flaunting obscenities on my bumpers."

She paused for a deeper breath, and Peter used the moment to tell her about her daughter's predicament.

For a short space Felicity's chest remained expanded, like a balloon full of water, and then it sagged, the water pouring out the hole where a naughty Cub Scout had poked it with a pin. She fell into a chair, gripping the telephone. Susan? Her baby Susan?

"Yes, ma'am. I'm sorry to have to say it so baldly, I wish there were a gentler way to tell you. But she's in a desperate situation and we're notifying her family. Your son David is flying down from Richmond."

Yes. David would do that. David thrived on crisis. Maybe that was why his marriage had failed. His poor little wife had thrived on placidity.

Felicity knew Susan. Knew her very, very well. Susan was a girl who shrank, who held back, who settled for the familiar every time rather than face the unknown. Look at the way she'd stuck with that rotten Roger, for no earthly reason that Felicity could comprehend except that the decision to leave him was too much for Susan.

A lot of things were too much for Susan. Susan was exhausted by any change in her jobs, by new prices on old groceries, by new hemlines when she had got used to other lengths. How would Susan handle a terrible situation like this?

Felicity did not know. She had absolutely no idea how her daughter would rise to this occasion. Or fall, as the case might be. "What are you doing?" she said steadily.

Pete told her about the local police, the SBI and the FBI.

About roadblocks and car alerts and helicopters and two-way radios.

"But you don't know where they are now?"

"No, ma'am."

"Very well, Peter. You were right to call. I don't use planes myself. Nor do I drive over thirty miles an hour. I have trifocals now and I simply have not adjusted well to them. However, I shall be there as soon as I can. There is a young man in my botany lab who loves to drive fast. I shall have him take me to Nearing River."

"How fast?" said Pete. It would be the icing on the cake to have the whole Lonergan clan kill itself off in traffic accidents. "Tell him not to exceed the speed limit."

"My goodness, you *are* law-abiding," said Felicity Lonergan. "Of *course* we're going to exceed the speed limit. Do you really think I would fiddle around on the roads for four hours when I can make it in two and a half?" She slammed the phone down on the Cub Scout and dialed the botany office.

Twelve

=====

I<small>T</small> was a paved road, wider than most, but it had a curiously unused look to it. No white lines on the sides or down the center. Grass had grown knee-high right to the edges of the road. A couple of pines, dragged to horizontal posture by last year's ice storms, were still bent across the road, waiting to catch any truck or van that tried to sneak under them.

A tired sign at the intersection read DEAD END.

"There," said Jerry Sam. "Turn there. We'll have the driving lesson there."

The little low Rabbit scurried under the ice-killed pines and followed the vacant road through meadows and woods. On the right was the shell of a very old gas station, the kind shaped like a carriage house, with the pumps sheltered under the overhang. On the left was a row of shuttered and closed cabins, the old-fashioned sort of motel. The drive circling past them was overgrown with a purple flowering grass, and the crepe myrtles, symmetrical sculptures that had marched around the drive, needed pruning and paring. Six little cabins and one slightly larger that must have been the owner's house. A very faded sign still hung over the larger cabin. SHADYSIDE REST. FAMILIES WELCOME.

It had been many years since Shadyside Rest had had any families to welcome. A picnic table rotted under towering oaks and the split frayed ends of a rope swing dangled from one of the huge limbs.

In the dying sunlight it was a pretty scene, but sad, like a grandmother left to while away her old age in a shabby nursing home. Susan passed by it gratefully.

Another hundred feet ahead of them the road stopped. A three-railed metal fence blocked passage, and through the scrub of trees and brush that had taken over beyond it they could see a four-lane divided highway going at right angles to their deserted road. Wild raspberries had matted over the guardrail. Traffic was speeding by only yards away, but it could have been miles. Susan could not penetrate the brambles. Through the raspberries she saw two blue flashing lights on a green sedan. Are they even looking for me? She thought hopelessly. Do they even know I exist? Roger probably won't call home tonight. And if he does and I don't answer, will he do anything about it?

"All right already," said Jerry Sam. "Nobody's gonna see us here. Okay, Susan old girl, let's change places."

She walked around the back of the car so she could look in at the child. It had fallen to the floor when she'd stomped on the brakes to avoid the pickup truck across the road back there, but fallen limply, still wrapped in the plaid car blanket. She could not tell if it was alive. She comforted herself that at least its little limbs and head were at comfortable angles. Twice she had begged Jerry Sam to let her tend it, give it liquid, but he had gotten so angry she thought the baby was safer forgotten. I don't know what to do, sweetheart, I don't know how to save you. She hated herself.

There was one self-centered thing she could do. She paused for a fraction of a second before opening the passenger door and sprung open the hooks of her earrings. Pulling them out tore the scabs that had already begun to form. Her ears were swollen and tender. She let the earrings fall in the dust by the car.

"Okay. Now. First gear first, sir," she said. "The car will sort of buck a little at first, until you get the hang of letting the clutch out evenly, but don't worry about it."

Across the hood on the driver's side was a dark-brown patch, blotchy and clotted. She had managed not to focus on it while driving, just as when she drove by an animal's dead body on the road she achieved a momentary blindness until she was past it. Now it stared at her. The blood had formed a pattern like a face, its features swarming and loose under the water, glaring at her.

She closed her eyes. I am sitting here in my car with a murderer. A murderer of little babies and cousins and complete strangers driving pickup trucks. The sun is going to set in that beautiful Carolina-blue sky while I sit here with my comatose baby boy and my box of marshmallow-filled chocolate biscuits to reward the murderer with when he finds the right gears. I haven't yet done anything right. There is a whole world out there full of sane and loving people and I haven't managed to signal one of them. I am going to die. He is going to be ashamed when he can't mesh the gears properly the very first try and he is going to hit me on the head with the shotgun and leave my body for the rats and—

Stop it! That baby is back there! I am not coming unglued. I am getting that child to safety. No matter what. No matter what.

She was calmer after her self-lecture. She complimented Jerry Sam largely for his efforts.

This time it had happened in slow motion. They had no fewer than nine witnesses in the cars stacked up behind the pickup in each direction. And they had all seen just about the same thing.

The driver was a small woman, barely showing above the dash of her very small car. The witnesses had all been struck by the size of the car. Next to the big American frames of their automobiles, it had appeared almost a miniature.

The woman had red hair. Dark eyes and very fair skin. It looked as if she'd had a scarf over her hair originally, a bright forest-green scarf, but it had slipped backward and was half in her hair and half on her shoulders. She was wearing outsize gold hoop earrings that were, said one witness severely, much too large for her small features. Her shirt was tailored, pale green, and she had on a gold necklace.

The cops marveled at the exactness of the description. It was the first crime they could remember where the witnesses had not been so mesmerized by fear that they'd been able to focus on the perpetrators.

"The girl was so scared herself, though," said one of the

men. He was a tobacco buyer, on his way home from the Wilson markets. "She was like petrified wood. Rigid. She even drove a little way with her eyes closed. Till the guy slapped her."

There had been only one man in the car with her. A farmer, high up in the cab of his truck, which was loaded with burlap sacks of tobacco for the market, had been able to look right down inside the car. "No sireebob," he said definitely. "There was not a third person in the car."

"You're absolutely sure of that? There couldn't have been somebody crouched down on the floor in the rear?"

"Are you kidding? That little bitty car didn't *have* a rear."

"Was there a baby? A little boy almost two, wearing green pants and a red and blue polka-dotted shirt?"

No. Nobody had seen a child. They would have noticed the clothing if it was as gaudy as that. There was absolutely nobody and nothing in the car except the girl and the man. "And cookies," added the farmer. "There was boxes of cookies all over the place."

"And the man," said a black woman who had had nothing to contribute so far except nods of agreement. "After he shot up that other man, and after he sat back down again, do you know what he did then?"

"No, ma'am," said the officer. "What did he do then?"

"He put a piece of bubble gum in his mouth and began chewing it."

"That's right," confirmed the farmer. "I remember that now."

"And then," said the woman, her huge eyes like white moons in her dark skin, "then he blew a bubble."

Now that's cool, thought the officer. That's Jerry Sam to a T. You murder a guy, you shove his corpse off your hood, and you sit back in your comfortable car with your chauffeur and you prove how cool you are. You blow bubbles with your bubble gum.

He did not think that Susan Seton was having a very good time. Nor did he think she would be in very good condition when—and if—they found her. Back on his car radio, he asked them to telephone his wife. Make sure she was okay. Tell her to lock the doors. Double-check on where the kids were.

It occurred to Roger that there might be some profit in the Susan situation. People thought about people who were in trouble. His name would be in the newspapers, his photograph with his strong arm supporting his sweet stricken wife. He'd be able to mention the incident to potential clients, explain why he was so frayed these days; they would respond with concern, they would remember him. Be less apt to turn away a sale. Poor Mr. Seton, you heard about his wife, didn't you, he's had so much trouble these days.

Roger got into his Buick, turned on the stereo FM radio, rotated his body until he was completely comfortable, and humming along with an old fifties love song, set off for Nearing River.

Yates shook his head. "Stay out of it, Pete. It's out of our territory now. Two counties to the east."

He could not just sit around telephoning Susan's relatives. He had to do something. Half of this was his fault anyway.

"It's not your fault," said Yates, annoyed. "You gave us the identification, didn't you? Listen. In a few minutes the Cape County force will have them anyway. First they had that call from Bros whatever his name was with the store and they moved every available car into the area and that meant they got to the James killing in literally only five minutes after it happened. Five minutes, Pete. Where can Hopps go in five minutes? They've closed off every single damn road in Cape County. It's just a matter of closing in on Hopps now."

"Unless he was already out of Cape County before they closed the roads."

"You know that didn't happen. The murder took place at the geographical center of the county. About eighteen miles each way to the bordering counties. Cape is one empty place. Not anything like the road network we got. They can shut it up tight like a clam."

"Susan got them away before," said Pete. He could not identify the heart of his unease. He'd run into amoral killers before. Maybe because he and Susan had been in school together. Maybe because he knew how terrified his own wife would be in her place. "What if they switched cars again?"

"Jerry Sam is too dumb. It was only dumb luck that got them this far."

"I can just see somebody getting trigger-happy when they corner Hopps, and Susan will be the one to get killed."

Yates had no retort for that. It had happened once last year, and the police department in the city where the hostage had been killed, instead of the criminal, was still under investigation. It happened. What could you say? The SBI and the FBI and the Cape County force had been warned and warned to be careful of the girl.

"Any report from the divers?" said another policeman, coming in.

"No," said Yates. "They said an hour ago that the water was really treacherous. They're getting up a lot of garbage, but no kids and no black plastic bags."

"We heard from Duke, though," said Bloom. "The little girl? Lindy? They think she's going to be fine. She'd been struck with something dull-edged and was concussed, but the bag actually saved her from drowning. Doctors are mostly just observing her, but they think it was a simple concussion with no aftereffects."

"All right!" exclaimed Pete. "That's great."

Yates shrugged. He didn't want to be the guy who drew the privilege of telling the Davenports that they had half the twins left.

"You know," said Pete, "I'm off duty."

"You back on that subject again?" said Yates. "I can't control what you do or where you drive when you're off duty. But you got a wife and kids to think of, too. Why do you want to go messing around with a gun-crazy maniac like Jerry Sam Hopps and maybe get yourself hurt?"

Partly, he supposed, because of Roger. Anyone going through the hell that Susan must be in deserved a husband who at least pretended to be interested. Pete felt he should give a damn about Susan to make up for Roger. And for having such a thought, he felt like a colossal ass. Romantic hooey.

"The brother is coming, you said," said Yates. "You be the one to go to the airport and meet the brother, long as you're so hot to be working today."

Pete didn't want to meet the brother.

"Somebody sure has to meet him. I'm not about to let him hop into a rental car and go charging off after his sister. Been enough of a massacre already."

"I can go meet him," volunteered Bloom.

Bloom was a good guy. Pete had always known it. Now he had proof.

"You're a jerk," said Yates mildly to Pete.

Pete shrugged. He had always known that too. Now they all had proof.

David Lonergan was an efficient, successful man. Once he had heard himself announce that he was going to charter a private plane, he set about doing it. Called the airport, made the arrangements, which turned out to be amazingly simple for him, at least—he didn't know what the pilot might have to rush along with—and drove quickly to the bank. He'd promised cash, and he had no way of knowing what other expenses would come up in Nearing River.

He compartmentalized his thoughts. In one section he placed Susan, maniacs, rape and time. He would not think about those things. In the other immediate section he put money, schedules and traffic between him and the airport.

He had been divorced for so many years now that he was long over the habit of reporting in to anyone. It was not necessary to call home and make long explanations. In three succinct sentences he told the other men in the office what was happening, to handle everything until he returned, and hurried out of the building.

He had never been in a small plane before. Trips to D.C. and New York, occasionally Atlanta, were common, but he just grabbed the easiest Piedmont or Eastern flight and went tourist. After the clutch in his stomach during takeoff he felt no nervousness and tried to enjoy himself. But he felt guilty even glancing out the window to see the patchwork of the countryside, so bright and perfect on this clear day, so he stared at the seat ahead of him and thought about Susan.

And about Roger. David wondered if they had been able to notify Roger. The man was always somewhere else. When Susan had had an appendectomy, Roger had been somewhere else. When the stove had caught fire and the kitchen curtains gone up in smoke and Susan had had to spend the night with neighbors, Roger had been somewhere else.

David's own marriage had been a disaster, and he tried hard not to be prejudiced about other people's happiness or lack of it just on the strength of his own bad experience. But he could not believe that his sister was happy. She had never talked to him about Roger; Susan was a private person. It was important to her to be a good hostess, to smile and provide quiet laughter and good conversation with a delicious meal. David had no way of knowing what was really between Roger and Susan.

He wondered if Roger would be annoyed to find David flying in like Richard the Lion-Hearted, sword in hand.

As long as it's cash in hand, Roger won't mind, thought David.

He knew Susan would be glad to see him. Under any circumstances Susan would come flying across the room, throwing herself into her big brother's arms, kissing and hugging with exuberant abandon. Under *these* circumstances—

He closed off his thoughts and looked down at a spidery network of swampy rivers below the plane.

Until they brought Timmy in, Laura James was in control. Her son walked up to his mother, his big homely face full of shocked concern, and she began to weep. "Timmy, it was so awful," she said, reaching for his hands, clutching them, rubbing them against her tear-soaked cheeks. "Why did we do it? Why did we try to find that terrible man? Timmy, it's all my fault. For caring about all my stupid furniture and dried flowers. That's why your father went after him. For me. Because my house was ruined. Oh, Timmy, Timmy, Timmy."

Timmy sat beside her. He did not think his daddy had gone out for her sake. C.D. had done it for kicks. He held his mother awkwardly. A few hours ago he had raged like a child in nursery school over his torn skateboard posters. Now he could not believe that he had ever even stood on a skateboard. That was for babies.

He had had to look at his father's body. Most of the buckshot had missed, they told him, or at that range Mr. James would have been torn in half. Hopps had apparently not even tried to aim his shotgun, just lifted it and pulled the trigger. Timmy wondered what his daddy had been thinking of, leaping out of his truck, waving his shotgun at a man he knew perfectly well also had a shotgun—C.D. James's own.

"I was crocheting," said his mother. "I shouldn't have been doing that."

"Why not?" he said reasonably. "You like to keep your hands occupied."

"Your daddy was getting killed and I was turning the edge of a ripple. It was a yellow row." She went on and on about the afghan. Timmy began to be frightened. He had no idea how to calm her.

The policewoman said softly, "I just called the hospital. They're going to take a look at your mother in the emergency room. See if she needs to spend the night. Shock, or something, I don't know much about these things. If she's all right, you two can go on home with your uncle. He's waiting outside."

Timmy found himself hoping the doctors would put her in the hospital. There was enough to think about without having to hug his mama all night long.

"Timmy," said the policewoman.

"Ma'am?"

"Stay with your mama now. There's been enough trouble. You don't try to help by going after Hopps yourself, hear?"

Timmy had never thought of it. Immediately the thought turned into a vivid image complete with plot and dialogue.

"Timmy," she said, reading him.

He smiled sweetly. "Of course not," he said.

. . .

Hollister Boudreau, product of a Boston Episcopalian mother and a French-Canadian Catholic father, was spending his college years busily rebelling against all that both his parents stood for. Since between them they covered most of the available territory, Hollister's choices were rather confining. Whatever would upset one parent, thus satisfying Hollister's immediate goal, was sure to please the other, thus ruining the point. He was reduced to pursuits like cross-pollination of exotic flowers and pot-throwing, on which topics neither Boudreau had ever expressed opinions.

He was seriously considering giving up the rebellion, and Mrs. Lonergan insisted that it was the wisest course. He consoled himself that both parents would hate the decision, since it had been influenced by a Southern woman and the Boudreaus were very suspicious of all Southerners.

"Ordinarily I'd be glad to," he told Felicity, trying to remember some phraseology his mother used when forced into white lies. "It's just that a motorcycle isn't the sort of contraption you'd be very comfortable on."

"Comfort is not paramount at this time, Holly," said Felicity Lonergan. "I am in a hurry."

"I can appreciate that," said Hollister. "It's a scary situation for your daughter to be in, but—"

"Holly, I know you have an extra helmet. I've seen it dangling from your Yamaha. I know you can carry a passenger because I've seen you hauling your girl friends on it."

He did not know how to tell her that she made three of his girl friends.

"Are you so puny you can't keep your balance with me

on the back?" demanded Felicity Lonergan.

"No," he said doubtfully.

"Then get your body and your cycle over here. We must rush."

He tried to think of anybody he knew with a good fast car he could borrow, but everybody he knew either drove a heap or didn't trust him. He wondered what Mrs. Lonergan weighed. The salesman had extolled the virtues of his bike—heavy, vigorous, strong, determined, et cetera. Well, Holly thought, I'll let the salesman know. I'm certainly putting it to the acid test.

Jerry Sam drove down the dead-end road for the seventeenth time, and for the first time he went smoothly from first to second to third. "What about fourth?" he asked.

"Fourth is for high speeds," said Susan. "We can't get up fast enough on this short a road. When we get out on the regular road again, I'll help you slide fourth in. Here. Stick it in neutral now. That's right, leave the clutch in, and practice going in and out of fourth. No, it's over more. A little more. No, you're in second now. Fourth is over here."

"Sir," corrected Jerry Sam.

She turned her smile on. "Sir," she repeated. "Fourth is — There you go! You've got it! You're learning so quickly, sir. It took me weeks to learn to drive this car. And we've only been here a few minutes. You're so clever, sir."

He loved it. His rat teeth showed between his lips for another one of his genuine simulated smiles. She shivered inside her belly and kept the beaming expression glued onto her face. "Jerry Sam," she said softly. She slid her hand off the gear knob and over to his thigh.

His jaw began to work back and forth. He focused on the dashboard. He swung his torso in a very slight rhythmic movement. Susan mastered her revulsion and said his name over again, as sweetly, as adoringly as she knew how. No one was going to save Susan Seton. She knew that now. But maybe Susan could save someone else.

"If you let me leave the baby at somebody's house," she whispered, "you and I could have a good time together. Go to a motel. You know. Just the two of us."

A motel would be safe. Room phones. Clerks that had to be paid before they gave you the key. Cars parked everywhere. Traffic on the roads.

Years ago, in another life, when she had been a teenager in secretarial school in Raleigh, she had been forced to attend a lecture on safety given by a Raleigh police officer. They had all been embarrassed. It was about rape. In those days you didn't even say the word out loud. You certainly didn't sit in an auditorium and listen to some big burly man say the word over and over again as if he were talking about eggs and ham.

"Balls and eyeballs," the cop said succinctly. Susan and her girl friends had squirmed in giggly embarrassment. That first word was a no-no. "Put your knee in the first and your thumbs in the second," said the cop, "and you'll be all right."

Susan had not even been able to bear the thought of gouging out someone's eyes. It would be so squashy and mushy. "But rape is a terrible, terrifying thing," said the

cop. "You are morally and legally justified in doing anything necessary to escape the rapist."

He had demonstrated how to bring the knee up with a
sharp jerk. Susan had covered her eyes with her hands,
ducked her head and burst into smothered giggles shared by
everyone in her row. The whole thing was too embarrassing
for words.

She was not embarrassed any more. She was angry. She
prayed that the anger would maintain its momentum.
Would allow her to carry through with whatever she would
have to do to destroy Jerry Sam. The baby comes first, she
thought. Once he's safe, I won't be so inhibited. I'll be able
to do something sensible.

"Just the two of us?" said Jerry Sam.

Her cheeks were trembling from the effort it took to
smile. And he wasn't even looking at her. He wasn't even
appreciating the smiles. She steadied herself, bit down on
the insides of her cheeks and glued the simpering expression
back on. "Just the two of us," she said. "Kind of a party. You
know."

Jerry Sam looked out the window on his left, away from
her.

"At some nice, warm, cozy motel," said Susan, trying to
hypnotize him with her smoothest voice. "All we have to do
is leave the baby somewhere safe. Then we can do anything.
Anything at all. Whatever you and I feel like doing. Together."

Thirteen

===

JERRY Sam drove. She cradled the baby in her arms. It was still warm, still lying oh so limply in her plaid car blanket. But it was alive. Don't let me be too late. Let him be all right. Let us find a house where people will act quickly. Don't let Jerry Sam renege on it. Please, God, be with me.

There was an inch of Coke left in the bottom of one of the soda cans. She trickled a few drops into the baby's dry mouth and saw with joy that its tongue reflex worked; it swallowed the Coke. Almost weeping with relief, she occupied herself helping the child drink. Drop by drop. She rocked him slightly, crooning unconsciously.

Jerry Sam drove slowly but competently. He had very little trouble with the gears, although once it took him so long to find third that the motor lugged as if was going to fall on the pavement. But it picked up, finally, and they drove along without problems after that.

Susan, touching the child's pretty little toes, was suddenly chilled by a new thought.

By now there were certainly plenty of police around, trying to locate the escaped convict. It had been an hour and forty minutes since Jerry Sam had murdered the man called Seedy. The cars that had watched the murder must surely have given a complete description of her Rabbit.

But. How would they know who she was? What if they thought Susan was an accomplice of Jerry Sam's? What if there were more roadblocks and the orders were shoot to kill? If Hopps's girl friend goes down with him, so what? How were the police to know that she was not some lover stashed away to help in just such an escape? How were they to know that Susan Seton even existed? That she was totally unwilling? If they connected her to the evasion of that other roadblock, where they had so inexplicably gotten away, they would surely believe her to be on Jerry Sam's side.

That would be the end, she thought, intending no pun. That would be the bitter end. I just can't stand it if the people I've been waiting to rescue me shoot me on purpose as if I were some dread female desperado.

She just had to get rid of the child. That was imperative. Anywhere—anywhere at all—would be safer than in this car.

"There's a house," she said. "What about that one?"

It was a squat wooden building set far back from the road. The setting sun was gentle to it, making it almost attractive. But it wasn't a very nice place. It was run-down, tacky, low-class. Who cares? she scolded herself. This is no time to be picky.

Her heart jerked. No telephone lines ran in to the house. No! This one is no good! What can I say to Jerry Sam? He's not going to take me around Cape County like a realtor.

"Nah," said Jerry Sam. "I don't like it. Kind of place where they'll come out with dogs and guns."

He drove on another quarter mile, where they saw a big old white house, very well maintained. Black shutters hung neatly around the windows. Tightly closed windows shining in the sunset meant central air conditioning, which in a house that size meant a hefty utility bill, which meant those people had money. "There," said Jerry Sam, "that's good."

He turned in the driveway and pulled up at their front steps.

Chrysanthemums spilled in sunset colors around the wide cement steps that led to the porch. Neatly trimmed privet and azalea ringed the porch, and at one corner a huge mass of daylilies, closed now, nodded greenly in a slight evening breeze. A wooden porch swing moved perceptibly. Through one of the windows Susan could see a light shining from a room farther back in the house.

They're home, she thought. Her whole soul seemed to relax.

"No funny business," said Jerry Sam. "I got my shotgun. You are going up to that front door and set the kid down in front of it. You can ring the bell and then you walk back here. You wait even two seconds for someone to come to the door and I'm letting you have it, you got that, Susan old girl?"

"Yes, sir." As quickly as it had come, the relaxation vanished. Her heart jackhammered in its prison of ribs. She was breathing deeply enough for three and her hands had turned to water faucets. She gathered the baby and its blanket in her arms.

"Hey," said Jerry Sam sharply. "Wait a minute."

Oh no. No, please don't find anything wrong now. Don't back out. Dear God, make him let me take the baby up to that porch.

"Where are your earrings?" said Jerry Sam. "What did you do with them?" He was enraged. His lips vanished, leaving a thin vicious line beneath his nose.

"My earrings," she said faintly. "Oh, sir, they were beginning to hurt me. I can only wear them a few hours, you know. Like contact lenses. I had to take them off."

He looked at her suspiciously.

"Besides," she said, summoning her sexy smile from some unknown reserve, "besides, those big old things would have gotten in our way."

Jerry Sam laughed. It came out flattened by his dreadful mouth, weaseling out around the corners of his teeth. "Go on," he said. "Get rid of the kid."

Carefully Susan got out of the car. The baby was quite wet. So far the blanket had sopped up most of it. She hoped these people would know enough to keep him warm. Call the rescue squad. Call the police.

She followed the path of piled pine straw and put her foot on the first step. Solid, thick, clean cement. She liked these people. They had a good paint job here. And those chrysanthemums. So warm and welcoming. Probably there was a vase full of the yellow ones on the dining-room table. Probably the phone was in the hall on a narrow-legged Queen Anne table. Just use it.

She crossed the porch and for one particle of a second she could not bear to set her baby down. *You wait even two seconds for someone to come and I'm letting you have it, you got that, Susan old girl?*

I've got it. I read you loud and clear. No problem.

She stooped, set the child neatly on a green rectangle of synthetic grass with a white plastic daisy in one corner. She had a footscraper just like that in front of their apartment. Hers and Roger's.

Roger. Susan felt a sudden slipping of her vision, like a child's kaleidoscope changing shapes. If she got out of this, she would end the marriage. She had put up with enough. There was more to life than wondering which girl was in which motel with Roger now. A lot more. She didn't like being a receptionist. Dr. Fiori was a nice fellow, but if she got right down to it, and Susan had never felt so completely like getting down to it, she hated dentists. They were all part sadist.

That wasn't fair. There were probably fine men in that profession. Dr. Fiori was a fine man. She forgave him for being a dentist. But she was going to do something else. She wasn't sure what. She'd always sort of wished she'd trained to be a nurse. Of course, it would take money to go back to school. She wasn't a little girl any more, with Daddy paying the bills. Susan felt as though today she had sped through adolescence, through her twenties, turned thirty and reached maturity at last. Today she was an adult.

She tucked the blanket around the little boy, straightened

up, rang the bell and listened for a split second to its loud peal. Inside she could hear voices. She took the steps in one jump and ran back to the Rabbit.

David Lonergan could not believe it. He absolutely could not believe it. "You can't do that," he said to Bloom. "I didn't fly down here just to sit around on my can. I won't stand for your interference."

"Sorry, sir, orders. You can talk to my superiors about it." Bloom wasn't worried. None of his superiors were available.

"Listen. This is America. This is not the USSR."

Bloom remembered something about that from school.

"You can't stop a man from driving where he wants to drive."

Bloom gave him a wide smile with his lips closed, the sort of smile that is friendly but adamant.

David fell back against the seat of the police car and sulked.

Pete Williams, driving his cranberry-red VW bug, reached Cape County.

Nearing River, he thought, isn't the most scenic place in the world (he had been in the Army and was acquainted with southern New Jersey and West Germany as well as eastern North Carolina), but it sure beats Cape County. Empty, spooky, unwanted countryside. But countryside was the wrong word. That sounded like fluffy sheep in the meadows and swallows swooping over barns filled with sweet-smelling hay. Cape County was dank, wet bog and pine wood. He had driven through it before on his way to the coast, but had never meandered on its back roads.

He didn't care for the drive now. The only reaction you had when you were in Cape County was to look at your map and gauge how long it would be until you were not in Cape County any more.

Twice he was stopped by cops. He felt like a fool. It was getting dark. He didn't know the terrain. He was in the way. They knew their jobs. This whole thing was pointless.

He turned around and headed back to Nearing River.

Felicity Lonergan sat very tall, gently holding Holly's waist. She had discovered a new love. When all this was over she would give up pottery. She was buying herself a motorcycle. This was the life. She laughed at the world, and the laugh was torn out of her mouth by the wind.

You're right, wind, she thought. Laughter is quite out of place. My daughter may be dead now. Raped or beaten.

Susan was so small. Felicity had never known what genes had combined to produce a child so petite. She wondered what size these Hopps cousins were. It did not matter. Two of any size could overpower Susan.

Don't you break down and cry, Susan Elizabeth Lonergan, said her mother fiercely. You are my daughter. You ride this out. You win, do you hear me? You win. That's an order.

Their name was Yearby. They had come down from Connecticut in 1927 when it became impossible to make a solid dollar in textiles there and rebuilt the mill in Cape County, remodeling along the way a big old country house that was the closest approximation to Tara that Mrs. Yearby could find. Textiles were a hard way to earn a living no matter what state you were in, but in spite of the unattractive swampiness of the town his grandfather had chosen, Pyke Yearby had no desire to live anywhere else or do anything else: the unions had not been able to find Cape County yet.

Pyke thought it might be because the roads were so poor. Or because there was no reason to drive through Cape County. Or because union organizers were afraid of the swamps.

Tonight he was in a good mood. A colleague of his in High Point (at less happy times Pyke referred to him as competition; at the least happy time, as a son of a bitch) had just won the latest round in the eternal battle of the union and it warmed Pyke's heart just to consider it. He and Cecile were drinking a toast in celebration.

Dusk was Cecile's favorite time. She felt no need to exert herself in any direction. It was the only time of the day when she did not feel wicked for doing absolutely nothing.

They were sitting in the den, which was the smallest and darkest and remotest room downstairs but which held the TV and was convenient to the kitchen, and in spite of the beautifully decorated parlor and library and dining room, they always ended up in the den, squashed together on the old chairs, staring at the crayon marks on the wallpaper left by children long since cleaning up their own children's crayon marks.

The doorbell rang.

"For heaven's sakes," said Cecile. "Who could that be?"

She didn't stir, but sat comfortably with her drink trying to guess who might be ringing her door at the dinner hour.

Pyke got up with an unnecessarily huge sigh and plodded toward the front door. He detested droppers-in. People had a wide nerve thinking they could just appear and be welcome. But he would smile heartily and beg them to come in and probably invite them for dinner and tell them to do it again sometime, he surely had been glad to see them.

Much to his annoyance, whoever it was drove off before he reached the door.

"I got up the minute you rang the bell," he said testily. He could see the car disappearing out of his driveway. It made an unusual sound, it reminded him of something, but he couldn't think what. "Get me out of my chair, ruin my mood," he said to the taillights, "and then be too rude to give me time to get there." He huffed to himself and went back to Cecile to finish his drink.

She had three separate plans going now.

The first was when they went in to register. You had to register at a motel. You had to park your car and get out and go into the motel office and pay ahead of time.

They had enough cash, they could pay cash. Or maybe they could put it on one of her credit cards. She would suggest that to Jerry Sam. It's saving you money, she'd say, smiling. Make my husband pay for this, isn't that funny? Jerry Sam would think that was funny.

He would have to leave the shotgun in the car. They would go in together to register. She would hit him with a lamp or with a Danish chair, which every motel had in its lobby, light and easy to swing. She might be small but she was strong. Tennis. She'd hit him with an ashtray or a telephone receiver.

But he might send her in alone. That would be fine. She'd just tell the man at the desk what was going on and—

And what if he didn't believe her? What if he dillydallied around, trying to verify her story? What if Jerry Sam, waiting in the car, got suspicious and came in complete with shotgun? Who would get killed then? Enough people had been killed. She couldn't lead the next victim to the execution. She had to arrange this so that nobody but Jerry Sam got hurt.

She heard that last thought going through her mind and caught hold of it. The sick taste rose in her mouth again, and this time it was horror at the beast that Susan Seton had become. She used to go for walks and be careful not to step on ants. She wouldn't use insecticides when a bee got in the office; she always managed to shoo it out the door with a folded newspaper. And here she was plotting how best to hurt a man. Furthermore, relishing the idea. Savoring the vision of that ashtray welding itself to Jerry Sam's head. Loving the idea of herself gripping the leg of a chair, lifting it, hurling it. Seeing Jerry Sam sprawled prone and unconscious or even dead on the floor of the motel lobby thanks to her.

The shame went away. It was going to be necessary, and that was that.

Now—what would she do if Jerry Sam left her in the car while he went in to register? Obviously she could flee. Could and would. But somehow, too, she had to prevent his rage from spelling death for any more innocent people.

For the first time it occurred to her that the shotgun might be empty. He had used it on the dog and on the car radio of the white station wagon. He had told her that so many times she'd wanted to scream shut up at him. Plus he'd shot the man Seedy.

Nobody could be named Seedy. She must have misunderstood. The way she'd thought that Powell's name was Pal at first. The woman had had a very thick accent and Susan had just misunderstood.

Anyway. That made three times he'd used the shotgun. Did it have pump action or had he been reloading it each time? She simply had no way to tell. She knew too little about guns. She just did not know how often—

I could use the shotgun, Susan thought.

It was an entirely new idea. She had not before visualized herself with the gun in her hands.

I wouldn't necessarily have to shoot him. I could just bop him one, the way he did Powell. I've already seen how well that works.

She saw the kudzu vine shivering in the wind, saw the tobacco shed with its sway-backed roof, the low door they'd kicked in so they could shove Powell inside. Rats. Had there really been rats in there?

This is no game, Susan. You are not shaking dice for your turn and moving around the Monopoly board. Jerry Sam will kill you. You promised him yourself and you promised it would be good and you either have to cut him off at the pass or it has to be good and those are the only choices, the absolutely only ones, because Jerry Sam is a killer and he likes to kill and this is no game.

The sun was disappearing behind the trees.

Zero hour.

Physiologically there's no reason why I can't be raped in the daylight. Well, it isn't daylight any more. It's nighty-night time.

Balls and eyeballs, said the cop.

If I'm reduced to that, can I do it? Can I really take my thumbs and stiffen the joints and ram them into Jerry Sam's eye sockets?

The sick taste filled her mouth, she was going to vomit.

Okay, you're okay, get a grip on yourself. We'll be at a motel before long and I can handle it, I know I can. Lights and people and other cars and somehow I will do the right thing.

She folded her hands around the strong comforting strap of her seat belt.

Jerry Sam turned right. It was another paved road, wider than most but with a curiously unused look to it. A tired sign at the intersection read DEAD END. Grass had grown knee-high right to the edges of the road. A couple of pines, dragged to horizontal posture by last year's ice storms, were bent over the pavement.

On the right was the shell of a very old gas station, its decrepit pumps sheltered under a rusting metal overhang.

Susan couldn't breathe. Her eyes glazed with fear.

In the center of the road, in the dust, were the tire prints from the Rabbit's last exercise.

And on the left, beyond a rotting picnic table and the split frayed ends of an old rope swing, was a motel.

Fourteen

===

I NOT only drive a Rabbit, thought Susan, I behave like one. Hopping along with my pink nose twitching. Hopping right into the trap.

Jerry Sam came to a full stop at the bottom of the circular asphalt because there was a slight rise and he could not manage it in third gear at five miles an hour. Slowly and carefully he shifted into first, and with a spurt of too much gas the little car jerked up the rise, crushing down the grass patches that had eaten into the asphalt. He scanned the selection of cabins and chose the fourth one. For a moment before he shut it off, the diesel engine idled, putt-putting softly.

"Sure hope they've still got beds in them," he said, frowning. "You don't suppose they cleared out the furniture, do you?"

She could not speak.

Jerry Sam pushed the square red release button and his

seat belt slid obediently back into its hanging position. He
arched his back, found his hip pocket and jammed the car
keys in it. With his left hand he opened the door.

Susan observed him remotely. She was no longer entirely
attached to her body, which was merely a thick vertical
piece of flesh bent in several places to conform to the seat
design but which no longer was joined to her mind or eyes.
Perhaps Jerry Sam was at the wrong end of the binoculars.
She watched him stand up on the grass. Her view of him was
a photograph framed by the open door: a male body from
the knees to a few inches above the waist. He hooked his
thumbs in the belt loops of his jeans and rocked twice on his
heels. Then he turned and began to walk slowly around the
front of the car.

Susan contemplated the size of her brain. She had thought
Jerry Sam so stupid. But she was the one with a brain the
size of a butter bean. None of her fine gaudy plans were
applicable. And her present brain, floating away from her
body in spite of the thick viscous thing it had become,
seemed no longer to function. Oh, there were thoughts in
it. Thoughts of the furniture, if any, still in the deserted
cabins. Mice in the mattresses. Snakes in the corners.
Thoughts of the sunset and how symbolic it was, how neatly
it would vanish just as her life went dark.

But she was unable to think of anything to do except wait
for the inevitable. In a way it was a relief not to have to
think. To surrender. To let her muscles surpass her brain in
slackness.

There was no point in trying to formulate another plan
anyway. No matter what she did, Jerry Sam was still so

much bigger and stronger than she was, he still had the shotgun cradled on his forearm, he still—

He didn't.

There was nothing on his arms but stolen T-shirt and short dark hairs.

The shotgun was still in the car, lying on the floor.

"Who was it?" Cecile asked her husband. She was eying her bag of embroidery, which was sitting on the floor next to the television. She never did handwork in the summer. Embroidery was exclusively a cool-weather pursuit. Suddenly she was eager to pick it up again. Her fingers itched for the needle. She could visualize perfectly the tiny brown nuthatches she had been working on last spring when she'd put the project aside.

"Don't know," said Pyke. "Drove off without waiting for me to get there."

"That was rude," said Cecile. She glanced at the clock. They could catch the end of one news program and the beginning of another if they turned on the TV now. But did she care what was happening in the world? Cecile doubted it. The same little countries would be having the same large troubles they'd had last night and the economy would be just as infuriating and all that would happen would be the launching of a huge argument about government interference in private enterprise, one of those shouting matches where she and Pyke were on the same side but got themselves so angry that they came to the brink of divorce yelling.

She decided against television. "Maybe it was United Parcel with a package," she said. "Sometimes they just ring the bell so you'll know to go and get it."

"No. Small car. Saw it driving away."

"Anyone we know?"

"If it had been, I would have said so."

"Of course," conceded Cecile.

"But that must be the explanation."

"What?"

"Somebody left a package. Are you expecting anything?" Cecile was forever in charge of something or other, which often entailed odd deliveries of toys for retarded children or donations for craft fairs or ticket receipts for the June Dance or whatever.

"No," said Cecile.

"Guess I ought to check," said Pyke, not wanting to repeat the hike to the front door.

Cecile was a generous person. "I'll go with you," she said, setting down her glass. "Maybe someone has left an invitation to join a textile-workers' union."

Pyke was not amused. Nevertheless they walked arm in arm to open the front door.

Wrapped very neatly in a green and red and yellow plaid football blanket was a baby. For a moment they gaped. When Cecile picked it up disbelief was quickly dissolved in a strong scent of ammonia. "It is definitely a baby," she said, "and it is very, very wet."

"A baby," said Pyke. "A baby!" It seemed to him that movies had been made about babies on doorsteps back in the thirties. Surely that stuff was passé. People with spare babies gave them to adoption agencies, where would-be mothers were lined up twelve-deep to grab them. Dazedly he followed Cecile to the kitchen.

"Some package," said Cecile. "Why, the poor little thing is all—" She caught her breath. The child was hurt. Badly. Bruised. Dried blood near its little eyes. Either asleep or in a coma. She had to rest her fingers on its little chest to feel a heartbeat; she could not see it breathe, but when she put her cheek against its mouth there was a tiny whoof of air. "Call the rescue squad," she said quietly. From the bottom kitchen drawer she got clean linen towels and tied an old-fashioned diaper around the little boy. In the downstairs bath she got a full-sized towel and wrapped him cocoon fashion in that. Then she filled a sponge at the sink with cool water and began dripping it in the child's mouth.

"How do you know to do that?" said Pyke, dialing.

"I don't know. But he's very dry. He needs fluids."

The rescue squad answered on the second ring. "This is Pyke Yearby," he said, giving his road and box number. "Someone just left a badly hurt baby boy on our doorstep. Can you send an ambulance?"

The squad answered in the affirmative, sounding as if deserted babies were all in a day's work, and that was that.

"Did they say how long before they get here?" asked Cecile.

"No." He was swept by a wave of love for his wife. She was concentrating totally on the white limp piece of child that lay across her kitchen table.

"Get out that paperback on medical emergencies," she ordered him. "It's upstairs on the bookshelf in the hall next to those gardening manuals. It's got a blue cover."

He marveled that she knew it so precisely. He was willing to bet that she hadn't touched that book since their children left elementary school. He took the steps two at a time. The book was just where she had said it would be. He came downstairs to the accompaniment of sirens.

My heavens, that was quick, thought Cecile. They must have gone a hundred miles an hour.

"It's not the rescue squad at all," said Pyke from the hall. "It's police." He stared out the front window. "It's a *lot* of police, Cecile. Must be five cop cars pouring up our driveway." It's a raid, he thought. But they have the wrong house. I don't have anything to get raided. I don't even grow marijuana in my kitchen garden.

In seconds his house was full of police.

No, Pyke had not seen who was driving the car. Yes, it was small. No, he could not identify it more clearly. Well. It had been—oh, at the most, four or five minutes from the time the car pulled away to the time they went out and picked up the child and then maybe another minute or two before he called the ambulance. And no more than two minutes before the officers had arrived.

They vanished from the house like some mysterious spring tide. Blinking, he tried to get answers from the one officer left him, in the kitchen watching Cecile watch the baby. "What's going on?" Pyke said, trying to establish himself.

"Kidnapping," said the officer. "We're pretty sure this is the baby we've been dragging rivers for. The kidnappers tried to murder his sister."

Cecile gasped and sat abruptly on the kitchen chair.

"May I use your telephone, ma'am?"

"Surely," she said.

He dialed eight numbers. Not a local call, then, but still within the area. "I'll pay you back the toll," he said.

"No, no. Think nothing of it," said Cecile.

The ambulance attendants came in the open front door and very efficiently collected the little boy.

Cecile hovered anxiously. "May I come?" she said.

"We'll call you when we get to the hospital and tell you what the doctors say, is that okay, Mrs. Yearby? We got to hustle and I'm afraid you'd just be in the way, no offense intended, ma'am."

"Oh," said Cecile.

The officer on the telephone was saying revealing things like "Right" and "Uh huh." Pyke and Cecile stood together, feeling silly and redundant. "What can I do to help?" asked Pyke.

The officer hung up. "Nothing, sir, we appreciate the offer."

"Who exactly are you looking for?" said Cecile.

"Two men and a woman they've kidnapped."

"Was that her little boy?"

"No, ma'am. I'm right sorry, but this is kind of an emergency and I got to rush off. 'Preciate y'all being so quick calling in." He beamed at them but the smile missed its targets; he was already out the front door and vaulting into his waiting car.

Fifteen

———

SHE gauged the obstacles. First she would have to remove her seat belt. Then turn around. Get up on the seat on her knees. Lean between the front seats. Reach around to grab the gun. Pull it through. Turn around once more.

By that time Jerry Sam would have strangled her twice.

She sat in renewed defeat. Jerry Sam opened her door. Leaning over her, he released her seat belt, guided it back, and taking her elbow, assisted her out of the car. "Thank you," she said.

Thank you?

The absurdity of it bubbled in Susan's throat, swelling, becoming laughter. Jerry Sam was actually tucking her hand into the crook of his arm, leading her across the grass.

He was escorting her to their honeymoon cottage. Perhaps the bed would be circular, with a tufted headboard and red satin sheets. Perhaps a thoughtful management would have delivered flowers and champale to the bedside table.

Her giggles poured out, breaking the calm of dusk like a flock of shrieking birds. "It's dinnertime," said Susan between giggles. "I'm awfully hungry, aren't you? Look under the oaks. A lovely brick fireplace. Let's go into town and pick up some steaks and some briquettes and have a cookout."

Jerry Sam looked at her as if she were crazy. She was impressed by the expressions his flattened skin could manage. To think she had once believed him featureless. "Are you crazy?" he said.

She laughed gaily. "Yes. I'm crazy."

She was totally disembodied now. A dancer wrapped in scarfs, leaping gracefully, dipping, pirouetting.

The laughter was in complete control. She stretched out her fingers to catch the cascading giggles, but they eluded her. Instead they caught on the branches of trees and echoed.

Popped my cork, she thought. No, no. Much too dull an expression. I must think of a better one. Something frivolous. Something gay and silly.

She was flitting around the crepe myrtles now, in and out, back and forth. "Look!" she cried. "Over there! Look at those beautiful weeds. That's where I came in, you know. To find weeds, armloads of weeds." She was next to him again. What strange choreography. To a symphony of crazy laughter. "Where are the scissors?" she said. "Shining sharp scissors? I need them to cut my weeds."

Jerry Sam looked at her uncertainly. "In the car," he said. "I put them under the rubber mat in the back."

"Oh, wonderful! I'm so glad you didn't throw them out.

I can't rip up the weeds, you know. They're quite tough. All that happens is I tear the weeds and burn the palms of my hands." She danced back to the car, the wild laughter a tubercular cough, tearing her lungs, damaging her throat.

Opening the car door was a mechanical action. It sliced through Susan's frenetic leaping like a slap and she was left staring at a dark rust-brown carpet with small rubber floor mats, a shotgun and a pair of scissors.

She took the shotgun and turned in silent deliberation. Her hysteria was gone.

Jerry Sam stood at the top of the drive with his arms folded, staring at her imperiously: I'm the king of the castle and you're the dirty rascal.

But she was king of the castle. She had the gun. As soon as her fingers curled around the metal she understood guns. They weren't like thumbs in eyeballs, they weren't part of your bones and blood. They were separate. Whatever they did was their concern, not yours. You could use them without batting an eyelash.

"Isn't loaded, Susan old girl," said Jerry Sam. He began walking toward her. "You tried to make a fool out of me."

"No," she said, "a corpse." She aimed the gun.

"Forget it, baby. It's got pump action, all right, but I pumped everything out. You ain't got nothing to work with."

She fired.

The gun clicked.

Jerry Sam pulled it out of her numb hands and threw it on the ground.

.   .   .

The October heat dropped rapidly, not at all like August or September heat which swirls all night trying to get in the cracks and ruin everyone's sleep. It was a time to be out on the porch, swinging slowly in the old-fashioned way, before air conditioning, when everybody had a swing and a fan and a long evening of nothing to do but watch the neighbors rock on their porches.

From the air Cape County was an ant hill and many of the ants sported dome lights on their backs. The ants squinted into the last rays of the sun. It was a dangerous hour. An hour when you could scarcely tell if it was a Rabbit or a Ford going by you.

What have you ever been in all your life, Susan Seton, but a failure? she asked herself, stumbling alongside Jerry Sam. His fingers cut into her arm. You failed in your marriage. You failed either to find or to succeed in that career twentieth-century women are supposed to thrive on. You failed to save four lives today. You failed to rescue yourself. You deserve whatever's coming. You earned it. You stood around in your total ineptitude and gathered in this reward.

The cabin doors had been locked by the simple technique of nailing small bits of scrap lumber across the jamb and the doors. The nails had worked their way out slightly, or possibly never been nailed down with much enthusiasm to start with, and were very rusty. The scrap lumber was rotted. Jerry Sam jerked at it viciously and the wood split. He kicked, stretching to reach so high, and it splintered, swinging in pieces from the nails. With his fingers he picked off the remaining shreds of wood and shoved in the door to the fourth cabin.

It had a vile decaying odor, as if Powell had transported his corpse there. Susan was shoved in. She could see nothing for the darkness. There were windows, glinting slightly, but the sun was too low to penetrate them. What's in here? she thought. Birds' nests? Rats? Snakes?

The shudders returned. They possessed her entire system. They coursed up and down her body like a harbinger of Jerry Sam's hands.

"I'm going back to get the scissors," said Jerry Sam. "I got an ear to cut off, remember?"

Only vaguely. There had been so many threats. She remembered the cats better. Poor hopeless strays he'd left mangled and dying by the railroad tracks.

She stood in the cabin, dully watching him through the open door. Her eyes grew accustomed to the dark and she saw that the owners had not taken the furniture. There was a large low shape that must be a cot. A taller thick shape would be the chest of drawers. A chair. The kind of kitchen chair that had a slatted back. She tried to sit in it, but it had had a rush seat and the seat was rotted through. The chair was nothing but firewood joined by a few spindles.

Jerry Sam bounded up the grass, scissors glinting in his right hand. The way he ran reminded her of somebody. Who did Susan know who bounded?

Roger. Roger runs like that, she thought. A kaleidoscope of her marriage meshed with the memory of this horrible day until the years of her adult life seemed no different from an hour with Jerry Sam. She was possessed by an anger as strong as the laughter that had swept her over the grass. Anger at the entire world. Anger at herself. Such a dumb bunny. Such a rabbit.

Jerry Sam's frame filled the narrow door, blackening the inside of the cabin. She hoisted the chair and began to hit him. He did not make a sound. Nor did she. The only noises were the chair pounding down on his body. It was a thick thudding sound. She did not stop until the chair had broken into so many small pieces that there was no longer one big enough for a handgrip.

She stepped over Jerry Sam.

Outside it was very dark. Susan walked unsteadily down the circular drive, past her car and out onto the dead-ended pavement. Sounds of traffic came to her from the blocked four-lane highway on her left and the country road beyond the ice-killed pines on her right.

Dragging, she headed for the country road. She wiped the tears from her cheeks and drew in a long, reviving breath.

Above her in the sky the first star had appeared. A tiny, glistening, impossibly beautiful facet from a hidden diamond.

No one saved me, she thought. I saved myself.

Her legs, stiff as wooden stilts, moved her away from Shadyside Rest. A hundred yards ahead of her at the peeling sign that said DEAD END, a car with twirling blue lights turned the corner.

About the Author

CAROLINE B. COONEY is a young North Carolina housewife and mother. Born in Geneva, New York, she grew up in Connecticut and is something of a Renaissance woman. In addition to raising her three children and running her home, she and her husband are partners in a computer programming firm, she plays the organ professionally in local churches, is active in community affairs, and writes. Among her published works are a number of children's stories and one juvenile novel, with a sequel under contract.